"Wha___ doin___

Joanna's voice was tremulous, her pulse racing with emotions too confused to sort out.

Michael looked at her with clear, cool control. "What am *I* doing here? Oh, no, the question is, what are *you* doing here?"

"M-my father asked me to stay and watch the house. He and Viv are on the West Coast this summer."

Michael's eyes narrowed. "Is that so? Well, for your information, my mother happened to invite me for the very same reason." His eyes were still the brilliant cobalt she used to admire so much, but something about them had changed. Now they harbored a coldness she wasn't used to, a cynicism....

"But that can't be!" she gasped.

"The hell it can't!" He yanked a shirt from the back of a chair and whipped it on. "And since neither she nor your father would be so insensitive as to invite the two of us here at the same time, one of us must be lying."

"So it seems," she retorted, vaguely wondering why he should consider anyone who brought them together "insensitive." You'd think *he* was the one who'd been used and two-timed!

Shannon Waverly is familiar with the East Coast setting she describes so evocatively in *A Summer Kind of Love*: she lives in Massachusetts with her husband, a high school English teacher. Their two children are both in college. Shannon wrote her first romance at the age of twelve, and she's been writing ever since. She says that in her first year of college, she joined the literary magazine and "promptly submitted the most pompous allegory imaginable. The editor at the time just as promptly rejected it. But he also asked me out; he and I have now been married twenty-one years."

A SUMMER KIND OF LOVE

Shannon Waverly

Harlequin Books

TORONTO • NEW YORK • LONDON
AMSTERDAM • PARIS • SYDNEY • HAMBURG
STOCKHOLM • ATHENS • TOKYO • MILAN

ISBN 0-373-03072-X

Harlequin Romance first edition August 1990

CHAPTER ONE

FROM THE STERN of the huge white ferry, Joanna watched the wharf at Woods Hole gradually recede and the picturesque southern coast of Cape Cod open out. The hot, sunny afternoon was fragrant with sea smells—fish and diesel fuel and salty spume. She took a deep breath and told herself to relax, that everything was going to work out for the best. But the effort was futile.

Leaning on the rail, she stared down at the churning water. Suddenly she became acutely aware of a weightless feeling in her stomach, a feeling of swiftly sliding backward, of water deepening perilously beneath her. Overhead, the large curved horn blared an ear-shattering farewell to the mainland.

Beside her, five-year-old Casey jumped, startled by the sound. But his fear passed quickly, and soon his attention was back on the sea gulls wheeling and swooping over the boat's wide wake.

Joanna could see excitement in her son's bright blue eyes. She could see it in the heightened color of his already tanned cheeks. And she smiled, remembering her own excitement the first time she made the six-mile journey across Vineyard Sound eight years ago.

But for her, that breathless feeling of being on an adventure was just a dry, detached memory. She wished she could recapture a little of it, and maybe she would in the restful, restorative days ahead—but for now she gazed at the sun-glitter on the water and felt nothing.

But then, she was used to feeling this way, this being stuck in neutral . . . finding no pleasure in the taste of food, making no emotional connection with music or sunsets or soft dewy dawns.

There was only Casey, the light of her life, the only reason she even bothered to get up in the morning these days. She had made innumerable mistakes in her life, but Casey would never be counted among them.

At the moment, he was holding half of a hot dog bun in his slender hand, wide blue eyes fixed expectantly on one particular sea gull. The gull, tame and trusting from following the ferry out to Martha's Vineyard every day, hovered over the outstretched morsel as if suspended by invisible puppet strings.

"Careful for your fingers, Casey," Joanna said softly. "Better toss it up to him."

She turned and looked for an empty deck chair, but it was early July and, as usual, the ferry was jammed with vacationers bound for the island. There were families of all sizes and ages, adventurous young people with knapsacks on their backs, a few unmistakable honeymooners.

Joanna sighed wearily. She had nothing in common with them. She felt isolated, exhausted, and so very old. Could it be that she was still just twenty-four? She felt a tide of apprehension rising through her nervous system. Was she doing the right thing? Six years ago, she had vowed she would never set foot on the Vineyard again.

But her father's invitation had sounded so tempting....

Dear Joanna,

How's my girl doing these days? Viv and I are fine—except for the fact that our lives have become rather hectic lately. My firm is opening a branch office in San Francisco, and I was told just last week that I'll be needed there to get the accounting department on its feet. I'll be leaving Boston the last week in June, which, alas, is just one week away. Viv has already gone—flew out to her sister's in Palo Alto as soon as she heard the news and, I hope, is pulling together an apartment for us somewhere.

We may be gone for as long as four months, which leaves us with a problem—namely, our cottage on Martha's Vineyard. We thought of renting it out, but neither of us really cares for the idea of strangers staying there. And a place left empty during the summer is just too much of a target for break-ins.

So I'm offering it to you, Jo. Though I haven't had time to discuss the arrangement with Viv, I'm sure she'd feel as relieved as I to know you were there watching over the place. Besides that, I think Casey would really enjoy it. My little grandson has never seen the ocean, has he?

But most of all, it would be a break for you. Phil's long illness and death last November were hard on you, maybe more than you realize. When I saw you in March, you didn't look well. You need a rest and a change of scenery. Staying in New Hampshire, living in the same apartment you shared with him, meeting friends who think of you only as half of a married couple—that can't be good for you. It only prolongs the time of mourning, which, in my opinion, you should begin to put behind you.

Think it over, Jo, and let me know your decision soon. I hope it will be yes.

Love, Dad

P.S. Our phone has already been disconnected so you'll have to write. Hurry.

The letter had come at a time when Joanna had been thinking along startlingly similar lines herself. Though Phil was gone, the visible framework of her life had changed very little. She still occupied the same apartment they'd moved into as newlyweds. She still went to work downstairs in her father-in-law's clothing store, which she and Phil had managed together. She still visited with the same family members and friends.

At first she'd considered this sameness a blessing, a reassurance that life would go on as usual and the transition wouldn't be too jarring for Casey. But recently she'd come to see it from an entirely different perspective. Everyone and everything in her life was now a reminder that Phil was gone. Ironically it was the very sameness of her surroundings that underscored the fact. At the shop, in the apartment, around her in-laws' Sunday table, someone was obviously missing.

And she was tired of it. As much as she had loved Phil, she'd finally got over the first, sharp pain of his death. And now she was afraid that the almost-comfortable sadness that had replaced the pain would never go away. If only she could make a break from it, get away from the people and places Phil had been so integral a part of. If only she could cut herself and Casey loose.

She'd hoped her son would be more resilient, but he and Phil had been too close. Usually a happy, talkative child, Casey sometimes became so sad these days, quietly sad. He occasionally wet his bed at night, sometimes cried disconsolately over the most trivial matter, and at times his chatter reverted to speaking about Phil as if he were still alive. "When Daddy gets home... Ask Daddy if we can..."

Joanna tried to take it in stride. She told herself it would pass. All he needed was time. But there were nights when it worried her to tears. How could she help her son through this traumatic time in his life? How could she be sure it would leave no emotional scars?

And then her father's letter had arrived. Her surprise was too obvious to hide. Her mother was visiting at the time and Joanna felt compelled to read it to her.

"Well, are you going?" Dorothy's lips tightened out of habit.

"Are you serious? I can't leave the shop now. The summer tourist season is just picking up. It sounds great but..."

Dorothy was pensive a long time. "Your father-in-law can survive without you for a few weeks," she finally said very unexpectedly.

"Maybe. But what about me? I can't afford a vacation!"

"How about the insurance money Phil left? Couldn't you dip into that a little? Your only expense out there would be food." Dorothy was a tireless, stiff-backed Yankee whose own life had inspired Joanna to be strong and independent, but it was obvious that even she believed her daughter needed a rest. And why shouldn't she? Joanna's hands shook so much, the teacup in them actually rattled.

"A vacation's just what you need," Dorothy continued. "It'll clear your head and calm your nerves. Even though I hate seeing you take anything from your father, I think you should go. Have a good time, too. You'll find everything easier to handle when you get back—Casey, your job, everything. I'm sure of it."

Everyone Joanna talked to agreed. Her father-in-law not only gave her the entire summer off, but he even insisted she take a small vacation bonus to help tide her over.

But now as the ferry chugged farther away from the mainland, she began to fear she had made the wrong decision. Not that her family was wrong in suggesting she get away from the sad tedium of her life. She knew they were absolutely right. But why here? Why did it have to be this particular island?

Of course, it wasn't their fault. Their intentions were good. How were they supposed to know about the devastation she had felt when she'd fled the Vineyard six years ago? She had hidden it so well. She'd returned to New Hampshire and acted perfectly normal, or as close to normal as she could muster under the circumstances. Then with her marriage to Phil following soon after, surely there was no reason for anyone to suspect that she was anything but perfectly happy.

And, truly, she *had* been happy! She'd had a wonderful marriage. She had become a successful working mother and an active member of the community.

With each passing day, the Vineyard had become more and more remote until there came a time when it seemed almost unreal, part of a dream she'd once had. She felt detached from it, detached from the naive girl she had been and, blessedly, from the people she had known. After that summer, she rarely saw her father and Viv anymore—only on those rare occasions when they chose to drive north to visit her—and she never again saw Michael.

Of course, she knew she'd be kidding herself if she said she never thought about him after that. Not that she chose to, or that it meant anything significant. But every so often a memory would blossom from nowhere, take her by surprise, and carry her back before she could push it down into the shadows of the past where it belonged. She didn't care about Michael or the Vineyard anymore. They meant nothing to her, and hadn't for years.

But now, as the outline of the island took shape on the horizon, fear began to whisper around her heart. What if this island proved not to be the cure for the dead weight in her soul? What if, after all these years, she discovered that it was capable of opening old wounds?

"Ma! Ma! He caught it! I threw it up and he caught it!" Casey's clear, sweet voice dispelled her dark thoughts. She looked down at his lean, angelic face, followed his gaze to the sea gull gliding away, and felt his excitement as her own.

"What a lucky sea gull, getting a hot dog for lunch!" Joanna laughed. "Okay, time to find ourselves a chair. We still have at least a half-hour ride."

Good-naturedly, he nodded and slipped his hand into hers. He was a slender but sturdy little boy with a meditative seriousness about his handsome features. Yet beneath that seriousness lay an engaging, congenial personality that had developed from spending so much time at the shop back home. Customers, leaning over to admire him, were more often than not drawn into conversation with him. A natural charmer, that was Casey. Just like his father, she sometimes thought.

They found an empty chair on the starboard deck, and Joanna lifted him onto her lap. "There it is," she said, pointing. "That's the island where Grandpa Scott's house is."

Casey leaned forward, eyes alive with curiosity. "It's so big," he exclaimed, causing Joanna to wonder if he was struggling with a cartoon preconception of what an island should look like.

"Yes, it is. Over twenty miles long."

"And there are trees . . . just like at home."

"That's right, babe. Houses, too. Whole towns of them. And there are farms and forests and beautiful windswept moors. I hope you weren't expecting palm trees and grass huts," she said with a gentle laugh.

Casey shrugged sheepishly, then leaned back. He snuggled closer, placid with tiredness. But that was only to be expected; he hadn't got much sleep the previous night because of his excitement. Joanna rested her chin on his silky brown hair and gently rocked him back and forth. Time passed, and when she looked down again, his long, dark lashes lay motionless on his cheeks. Softly she kissed him and returned her gaze to the approaching island.

It was going to be a wonderful summer, she told herself adamantly. They would sleep late and eat well and turn as brown as berries on the beach. And at the end of August, she would return to New Hampshire revitalized and ready to pick up the reins of her life once again.

Still . . . Joanna felt a tremor in her nerves, a tremor that had nothing to do with the engine's vibrating grind. That sense of gray-green water deepening perilously beneath her filled her soul. And though she knew perfectly well that the boat was moving forward, there was that unshakable feeling of sliding back. . . .

JOANNA MADE HER FIRST CROSSING over Vineyard Sound when she was sixteen, just out of her second year of high school, all legs and arms, with a thin silver brace across her teeth, and her blond hair cropped too short for her gangly height of five feet eight.

She was nervous and quiet and perhaps a bit angry, too. Her parents had been divorced when she was four, and she barely knew the handsome man beside her who was her father. Jim Scott had initiated the separation, leaving his wife, Dorothy, in New Hampshire for a glamorous socialite named Vivien Malone whom he had met while attending a business conference in Boston.

Although Dorothy had been upset by the divorce, she was a proud, stubborn woman who bottled up her pain and refused to let the world see that she was made of anything but fierce independence. She never remarried and never took support. She worked doggedly and raised Joanna alone, allowing her "conceited, playboy husband" very few visitation rights. And never with "that woman"!

"I don't know what ever possessed me to fall for a man like that," Joanna remembered her mother complaining even when she was too young to fully understand. "He was too handsome for his own good—that was the trouble." Dorothy would slap her steam iron onto the board with brisk, angry thrusts as she spoke, and the impressionable Joanna, sitting by the fire with her books, would take it all in. "Handsome men get used to women coming easy. If they get tired of one, they can just toss her aside and go find another."

Then, putting down the iron, she would lean over the board in the same way their minister leaned over the pulpit when he was about to warn the congregation about the snares of the devil. "Watch out for the really handsome ones, Joanna," she'd say, her thin lips tightening until they disappeared. "They'll break your heart every time."

Physically Joanna was like her father. She had, as her mother phrased it, the same wild, Irish green eyes and thick yellow hair. She had his saucy cleft chin and clever little smile. "But, thank God, you don't have his reckless nature, Jo. You're a good girl, a sensible girl. I've seen to that."

Jo was also a very perceptive girl, and though her father went out of his way to give the opposite impression, she knew that his new wife, Vivien, couldn't have been more pleased by Dorothy's refusal to let him visit or support his daughter. Joanna sensed that Vivien wanted him to make a clean break with his past and immerse himself completely in his new life in Boston. There he had everything a man could possibly want—a beautiful wife, the right country club, an established circle of well-to-do friends, even a son from her first marriage. As far as she was concerned, Joanna and Dorothy had simply dropped off the face of the earth. Joanna often heard a hesitation in her father's voice when he called, just enough uncertainty to convince her that Vivien treated any reminder of their existence with cold displeasure.

Considering the bitter feelings harbored by the adults in her life, Joanna was amazed that she got to meet Vivien and Michael at all. But she did, finally, that summer when she was sixteen. In addition to their home in Boston, Jim and Vivien owned a vacation cottage on Martha's Vineyard off the Massachusetts coast. That particular year, Jim had four weeks in July free and called quite unexpectedly to see if Dorothy would allow Joanna to join them.

"Do you want to go?" Dorothy had asked.

"Not very much."

Dorothy controlled a smile of satisfaction. "Well, I guess it doesn't matter then. Perhaps you ought to—show him what he's missed out on all these years."

Joanna arrived prepared to have a bad time. She knew Vivien didn't like even the *idea* of her, and she knew she wouldn't like Vivien. And she didn't. Vivien was so unlike her mother. She was youthful and tanned and energetic. But then, why wouldn't she be? The most strenuous thing she did all day was play golf with the other uppity people from Boston who summered on the island.

And her father? Joanna made an honest effort to like him. But her mother had been right. He was a bit taken with himself, and he flirted embarrassingly with every woman he met.

But Michael, Vivien's son? Michael had elicited feelings from her that made the rest of her feelings pale in comparison. She'd always resented this unknown Michael for usurping her place in her father's life. But now she was glad she could hate him simply for what he was—which was everything her mother had always warned her about in the opposite sex. He was too ridiculously good-looking for words, and he obviously knew it. He was smug, self-assured, and willful. Why, when she arrived, he was on the phone with one girl making lame excuses for having been at the beach that day with another. And the way his blue eyes glittered, she knew he didn't feel a bit of remorse for the deceit.

In his bare feet and blue swim trunks, with a towel flung negligently over one shoulder, twenty-year-old Michael stood about six feet tall. Though not the muscle-bound type, he evidently took pride in keeping fit. From the corded muscles of his legs, Joanna guessed he did a good deal of running. And he was tanned to the smoothest, deepest gold she had ever seen.

His hair, thick glossy brown, curled around his face with attractive abandon. Although he was indoors, he wore a pair of amber-tinted glasses—for effect, Joanna decided, eyeing him with open contempt. His mouth was smugly turned into a small, rakish smile, and when he spoke his voice was a deep, soul-moving baritone.

"Michael, get off the phone. Joanna's here," Vivien said. Then she sighed in mock exasperation. "My son, the lady-killer!" Joanna had no doubt he believed it.

From the very first day of her visit, Joanna and Michael argued. In retrospect, she had to admit she'd started it, but she couldn't help herself. There was something about Michael Malone that made her lose her composure and forget that she was shy. Perhaps it was the way his glittering cobalt eyes continually mocked her...or the arrogant way he went on about his precious Yale...or maybe it was simply those supercilious tinted glasses worn on the tip of his straight, suntanned nose. Whatever the reason, for the entire month she was there, they were entrenched in warfare. They short-sheeted each other's beds, sabotaged phone calls, threw jellyfish down each other's shirts, laced drinks with Tabasco sauce—in short, mocked and teased each other till Joanna was often reduced to tears and Michael was livid with cursing.

Never had she hated anyone so much in her life. He was the most infuriating, arrogant, self-satisfied chauvinist she'd ever met! To make matters worse, girls seemed to find him irresistible. The phone rang constantly for him, and some long-legged beauty was always "just pedaling by." Joanna couldn't stand it! How could such stylish, mature girls be so dumb? What disgusting line was Michael feeding them?

Before she realized it, though, her month on the island was over.

"Well, did you have a nice time?" her father asked as they waited at the dock for the ferry that would take her back to the mainland.

"Yes." Much to her surprise, it was the truth. Michael, who had opted to join them, looked up sharply from his book.

"Nice enough to come back next summer?" her father continued.

"Yes, I'd like that very much."

She didn't know why, but she felt oddly drained of the resentment that had filled her on the trip out. Not that she felt any real closeness had developed between herself, her father, and Viv, but they'd managed somehow to get along fairly well. She hadn't planned on matters turning out that way; they simply had—naturally, spontaneously.

And suddenly she knew the reason. Michael! She'd spent so much time conniving ways to get back at him that there hadn't been any time nor energy left to resent her father and Vivien. Michael had monopolized all her waking thoughts, become the focus of all her emotions, and without realizing it, provided a vent for all her pent-up anger. And now, as she stared into those clear cobalt eyes, she saw a joy and

a caring that she hadn't detected until then, and she knew
he had let himself be that vent all along.

The five weeks Joanna spent on the island the following
summer were as different from her previous visit as day is
from night. By some unspoken agreement, she and Michael called a truce to the teasing and pranks that had
characterized that other stay. Now was a time for them to
get to know each other and become friends. They swam
together nearly every day, rode bikes over hot, lazy back
roads, paddled the old rowboat around the pond, dug for
clams, shopped, cooked together, read, talked—especially
talked!—out on the sun porch late into the night, about
literature and astronomy, music and politics.

Ironically Joanna felt she knew Michael better than
anyone else in his life did, including the girl he dated most
often these days, Bunny Wilcox. Because she lived with
him, Joanna had time to discover his serious side. Michael
was not just the lady-killer his mother liked to dub him; he
was also a very intelligent and intense person, an idealist, a
dreamer. That summer, Joanna grew in utter awe of him.

Yet as close as they were, there was one subject they just
couldn't discuss in any depth. That was their love lives.
After all, she had seriously dated only one boy back home,
her best friend and devoted admirer since the fourth grade,
Phil Ingalls. And her relationship with Phil had never become more heated than a few innocent sessions of kissing
at the drive-in. While Michael…well, Joanna had a hunch
that Michael was sleeping with Bunny Wilcox…maybe had
even slept with some of his admirers the previous year. It
was a hunch that lingered even after he'd laughingly told
her she was fantasizing, even after he got angry and accused her of confusing him with her father.

Joanna tried to be cool and mature about it; Michael *was*
twenty-one, after all, and such behavior *was* commonly
accepted. But she found it hard. Michael was the most attractive, intelligent, virile young man she had ever met. And
late into the night, as the sea rocked outside her window,
she would lie on her bed awake, wondering where he was,

what he was doing. And her body rocked with a hunger so deep and inexplicable it brought tears to her eyes.

Again time passed too quickly, and again she found herself saying goodbye on the Vineyard Haven dock.

"Goodbye, dear," Vivien said, giving her a cool peck that mostly missed her cheek.

Then her father hugged her. "Write often," he said.

And finally there was only Michael, standing a little apart, watching her with a sad stillness in his eyes. His thick, dark hair, sun-streaked lighter brown across the brow, tossed in the breeze. She stepped up to him and held out her hand, swallowing a flood of emotion she didn't quite understand.

"Well, knock 'em dead at school this year," she said, feigning a lighthearted spunk she hardly felt.

He took her hand and held it tight. His blue eyes, dark with confusion, raked over her smooth, suntanned face, over her white-gold hair that now reached her shoulders, into her bright, Irish green eyes. In one year, he'd told her recently, she had grown from an awkward girl into a beauty.

He nodded and whispered, "You, too, kid." Suddenly he took her by the shoulders and kissed her cheek. She hugged him briefly, self-consciously, then turned as the deep horn on the ferry blasted its warning to come aboard. She grabbed her suitcase and ran, blinking away tears.

"Watch out for the real handsome ones, Jo," her mother's words had echoed through her mind. "They'll break your heart every time."

Michael wrote to her all that winter. Dorothy was furious and threw out the letters if she happened to get to the mailbox before Joanna did. But Joanna salvaged most. They were long, well-written letters, even poetic at times, filled with detailed descriptions of his last days at Yale. Joanna looked forward to them as if they were new installments of a serialized novel coming to her through the mail. In them she could almost hear his deep, melodic voice, feel the summer sun as if he were talking to her on the beach, smell the clean dampness of his hair.

Joanna was, of course, in love with Michael. The fact could no longer be denied. She loved him and probably had from the moment she'd laid eyes on him. And all the warnings from all the wise women who'd ever been jilted could not change her feelings one iota.

And then his final letter arrived and her joy was almost too much to bear....

Dearest Joanna,

This will be brief since I have to be out of the dorm tonight and still have my packing to do. Just wanted you to know I've won the fellowship! So it's off to Virginia in the fall, graduate work, a teaching assistant's position . . . life is too good at the moment.

Best of all, though, is that in a few weeks we'll be at the cottage again. Please stay the whole summer this time. I've missed you—more than you know or I'll ever understand.

No, I haven't seen Bunny, not since Christmas vacation when our two families went down to St. Thomas. She's written, though, and called a few times. I'm afraid she still isn't taking kindly to our breaking up. But there's no going back, and it's high time she realized it. Though I admit she once was a serious girlfriend—my *first*, let me repeat—I now realize my feelings for her were at best only tepid, lukewarm compared to what I'm beginning to discover with you.

Please, Jo, stay the whole summer. This one belongs to just you and me.

And so they'd had their romance. Joanna had loved Michael deeply that summer, and for some strange reason she'd let herself believe he loved her, too. And why not? He had told her he did, time and time again. He said he'd never felt closer to anyone before in his life and that he'd never let her go. He felt married to her—wasn't that how he'd put it?—married in a spiritual, mystical way that was far more binding than a civil license.

Now, as Joanna stared ahead at the approaching island, her heart swelled with contempt. What a pack of lies that had been! What a manipulative sham! But by then Michael had had years to practice his lines. He'd become a master at it, smooth-talking her into the most ego-shattering experience of her life.

She had turned a deaf ear to all her mother's warnings, had ignored her own hunches, too. All she'd heard that summer were the words "I love you," and she had let herself believe their summer, hers and Michael's, would never end.

But it did. Oh, lord, did it ever! In one bitter, definitive night. In spite of the calm perspective she had acquired over the years, Joanna still felt a little sick when she thought about it....

It was already the end of August, and she and Michael were facing yet another separation. Soon he would be heading for Virginia, and she'd be starting college in Vermont. She was sad—but hardly worried; after all, Michael had assured her it would only be a temporary separation till the day when nothing would keep them apart.

They were playing a game of Scrabble out on the porch when her father put down the phone.

"That was Peter Wilcox," he said, coming to the door.

"Bunny's father?" Joanna asked casually. The Wilcoxes were long-time friends of Vivien's from Boston who also summered on the island.

"Mmm. He wants us to stop over for a visit tonight."

"I'll beg off, if you don't mind," Michael said, catching Joanna's eye meaningfully. He had been right about Bunny's not taking too well to the idea of their breaking up.

"Mike, don't argue. He requested that you come along. It's 'imperative,' he said. You know how he talks." Jim tried to laugh, but there was no mirth in his eyes.

Michael took a deep breath of irritation. "Jo, do you want to go?"

But Jim cut in before she could answer. "I think Joanna had better stay here."

Joanna was too worried to be hurt by the snub. Something was wrong. She felt it in her bones.

By the time they returned, hours later, she was beside herself with worry.

"Where's Michael?" she asked warily.

Jim's brow was deeply furrowed. "He's... I think he went for a walk."

"At this hour?"

Vivien looked a bit more composed. "Jim, this is really none of Joanna's business. It's a private family matter."

"Vivien!" he admonished softly. "Come on, Jo. Let's go sit where we can talk more comfortably."

When they were seated in the living room, Jim wasted no time. "Joanna, Bunny Wilcox is pregnant."

"Bunny?" Joanna gasped. She'd first met the girl two years earlier... a spoiled, fiery-eyed brat, Joanna had decided then, an opinion that time had only confirmed.

"She claims the baby is Michael's."

It took a while for the words to sink in, but when they did, Joanna laughed. "That's preposterous!"

Vivien sighed resignedly. "I wish it were. But Bunny is definitely pregnant. She went for a lab test last week."

"Is that so!" Contempt sharpened Joanna's tone as she recalled all the times she and Michael had just happened to bump into Bunny that summer. "And how does she intend to prove who the father is, anyway?" She shook her head in disgust. "That's the oldest, stupidest trick in the book! She'd do anything to get her mitts on Michael. Boy, I thought she had nerve before, but—"

"Joanna, please! Have some compassion. The poor girl is distraught over her situation!" Vivien said.

"Oh, I bet! I can just see her now, crying in front of you people and then laughing up her sleeve. Tell me, what did Michael think of all this?"

Jim was about to say something, but Vivien caught his eye sharply. "He's going to marry her, of course," she answered smoothly.

Joanna's mouth opened but suddenly she felt so sick her words withered on her lips.

Jim drew himself up with a deep sigh. "Honey, I know there was something between you and Michael this summer. You tried to hide it, but we're not blind." He was compassionate but still he sounded as if he were talking to a child, as if he didn't consider her "something" significant. "Right now you're probably feeling as if this is the end of the world. Believe me, Viv and I understand."

Joanna shot the woman an alarmed glance. There was a strange, satisfied curve to her mouth.

"Though you may not believe it now, you will recover. Life *will* go on," her father continued. "Before you settle down with the man of your dreams, you'll have a dozen summer romances. You're so young. There's a whole world out there waiting for you. Forget about Michael and don't look back."

Joanna stared at her father stupefied. "What are you talking about, forget about Michael?" she whispered shakily. "He and I love each other."

Jim shook his head sadly. "No, honey. Michael is going to be a father. Don't you understand what that means?"

Joanna continued to stare. "But it's impossible. He can't be the father. He broke up with Bunny ages ago—last fall! *We're* going to be married!" she said feverishly. "We've got it all worked out. In a few years after he finds a permanent teaching position, I'm going to transfer to his school. Then..."

Vivien dropped her hands in exasperation. "Jim, this is too much! The girl is talking nonsense now." And then turning to Joanna, "Listen, I don't know what that son of mine led you to believe, but the idea of you two getting married...why on earth...I mean, I'm sorry if he led you on...." she stammered.

"He didn't!"

"Let me put it to you bluntly then. Michael and Bunny have dated for years," Vivien insisted almost impatiently. "I'll admit he's seen other people from time to time, but he's always gone back to her. The Wilcoxes are close friends of ours. We saw this coming long ago. I can't say I like the conditions under which they're getting married, but I know they'll make a go of it. They're such a wonderful match!"

Joanna was shattered with grief. She ran to her room and cried the night away. How could such a dreadful thing be happening to her? It had to be a mistake. She and Michael loved each other. They belonged together as no two people on earth had ever belonged before.

But evidently it was no mistake. Bunny was pregnant and Michael had agreed to marry her. Evidently he'd still been seeing Bunny on the sly, even while pretending Joanna was the only girl in his life. Evidently he had lied when he said he loved her. Joanna had meant nothing to him, nothing but a casual summer romance. How could she have been so blind?

She felt betrayed and defiled. All the times they had been together came flooding back to torment her. She felt used, degraded—and ultimately enraged.

She waited all night but he never came home. Too cowardly to face her, she decided. At five o'clock she washed her puffy face and packed her bags. She refused to stay on the island even one more day. In fact, she hoped she never saw the place or Michael's loathsome face again!

As she packed, her hands trembled. Inside, she knew something innocent and vital had died. Yet, oddly enough, she felt new strength rising from her desolation. In one night she seemed to have grown years older and wiser. Even her face, she thought, had lost its youthful openness and become more cynical.

She would go home to her mother now, back to a woman who had known all along what life was all about, back to Phil whom she had ignored too long, back to the friends and town where she belonged.

"CASEY! Casey, honey, wake up," Joanna coaxed gently.

The child lifted his head from her shoulder and looked around in momentary confusion.

"We're almost there, on Grandpa's island. We have to go to the car now. The ferry will be at the dock in a few minutes."

Casey slid off her lap and she rose. Her legs felt like rubber but she refused to admit it was anything but fatigue.

The car bin of the ferry resounded with the thunder of starting engines. Slowly Joanna inched her red compact forward, keeping an eye on the other cars also pressing toward the dock ramp. Casey had forgotten his tiredness and was now bouncing in his seat with excitement.

Before long, they were out in the bright sunlight and driving up the main street of Vineyard Haven. Passengers who hadn't brought cars were already crowding into bicycle and moped rental shops or gathering at the corner to wait for the tour bus.

Joanna paused at the intersection, unsure of which route to take. She loved the long coastal road, but Casey had done enough traveling for one day. She shifted the car into gear and set off on the quicker route through the quiet, rolling midlands.

How well she remembered her way—the roads, the old houses, the stone-walled fields and woods. Everything seemed so unchanged, so unfairly timeless. The knot of apprehension she had been denying all day tightened in her stomach.

As they got closer to the ocean side of the island, the air became slightly cooler and damp. She turned off the main road and down a narrow, rutted lane.

"We almost there?" Casey inquired, stretching his seat belt until he was kneeling up.

"Almost."

They dipped into a hollow, then climbed the crest of a hill. Suddenly a breathtaking vista opened out. Breakers were rolling in on a white sandy beach devoid of people as far as the eye could see. Casey gasped.

"That's South Beach, Casey. Isn't it super! And that's the Atlantic Ocean."

South Beach was a barrier beach, its surf-pounded sands holding in the waters of great inland ponds. The cottage stood on a gentle rise above one of those ponds. It was a typical 1920s New England summer cottage, with deep screened porches front and back, shingles weathered to a soft silver-gray, and wild roses spilling over its fence. All around it, the land dipped and swelled in meadows of beach plum, bayberry, honeysuckle, scrub oak and wildflowers. The air was heavily scented with their perfume.

Joanna pulled into the driveway and stopped at the front steps. "Well, this is it."

Casey leaned on the dashboard and looked up at the house. "I like it very much," he said with adult seriousness. Then his face broke into a smile. "Does Grandpa have a sailboat?"

Joanna followed his gaze out to the pond behind the house. A dozen white sails glistened in the late-afternoon sun. She smiled. "No, babe. He only has a rowboat, and I'm not even sure if that's in the water this summer."

Her gaze returned to the house . . . to the porch . . . to the front door that waited for her to enter. It had been six years since she'd been here, six happy and full years. Why, then, was she letting herself get so upset? Why these nameless anxieties?

So what if she and Michael had had a fling here once upon a time? So what if it had ended messily and she'd been hurt? All teenagers had to expect some heartache along the way. Big deal! She got over it.

She had started life in earnest after that—marriage and motherhood and working in the adult world. And now she was coping with widowhood. Michael was insignificant compared to the rest of her life.

He and Bunny had married that autumn and moved down to his campus in Virginia. A perfect match, Vivien had said . . . as happy as could be. And, of course, he was brilliant. And, of course, they had the most darling house and, of course, an exciting circle of friends. Joanna was sure if it hadn't been for a slip of her father's tongue, she never would have found out about the miscarriage.

After that, there was no more news. Dorothy, intercepting a phone call one day right after Casey's birth, had ordered her ex-husband not to bring up that "family trash" anymore; Joanna didn't need it.

Joanna supposed she could have asked how Michael was doing. But she never did. Her stubborn Yankee pride would not allow it. Besides, it wasn't too long afterward that Phil's condition was diagnosed and she had more pressing matters on her mind.

Well, it didn't matter now. One brief summer her life and Michael's had become entwined, then they'd gone their separate ways. Six years had passed, and time had put things into wonderfully calming perspective. She refused to let futile memories resurface and interfere with the healing she and Casey so badly needed. This was not a summer for looking back. It was the beginning of the rest of their lives.

"C'mon, Casey. Let's grab our bags and go inside."

Up on the porch she rummaged through her purse for the key her father had mailed her and inserted it into the lock. But suddenly, just at the touch of her hand, the door swung in.

Joanna stood on the threshold dumbfounded. "What on earth?" she whispered. With a frown creasing her brow, she stepped into the hall. All was quiet, everything in its place—the yellow rain slickers on their pegs, the fishing rods in the corner. Still, that did little to alleviate her fear that perhaps someone had broken in. She edged into the kitchen. "Anybody here?" she called timidly. Casey glanced up, sensing her apprehension.

"It's okay, Case," she soothed. "Want to take the grand tour?"

He nodded but reached for her hand as a precaution anyway.

"You're going to get a kick out of this place. Look, here's the living room," she said, leading him into a large, comfortable room paneled in knotty pine. A brick fireplace, at the center of the house, flanked one wall. Over it hung an antique ship's bell that chimed every hour. A glass-topped lobster pot served as a coffee table in front of the deeply cushioned, sand-colored couch. Carved water birds graced a shelf under the windows.

If someone had broken in, surely those birds would be missing. But, no, the room was the same as it had been the last time she saw it. The very same.

Joanna found herself staring at the club chair where she'd sat that long-ago night while her father and Viv told her about Michael's cruel deception. Suddenly it was as if she could see through time, see herself sitting there, confused, vulnerable, and utterly crushed. She shook her head and with a conscious effort brought herself back to the present.

"And through this door we have the dining room—my favorite." The room contained a large oak table and eight Windsor chairs, a Victorian sideboard cluttered with as many seashells as dishes, and walls hung with a dizzying assortment of barometers, bells, and seascapes painted by local artists. As she passed the phone table under the stairs, Joanna's memory inadvertently flashed a picture of Michael talking endlessly to some girl. Her smile wavered. Damn these ghosts from the past! They were everywhere she turned.

"And see this door, Case?" she said. "It leads right back to the kitchen."

Big blue eyes looked confused. He let go of her hand and crept in. Soon he discovered the pattern, that the rooms were clustered around the fireplace and that he could skip from kitchen to living room to dining room and back to kitchen again in an endless circle.

While he was getting acquainted with his surroundings, Joanna opened the door that led from the dining room out to the back sun porch. Facing the pond, the porch was a cheerful, breezy place, filled with an extravagant collection of wicker. But as Joanna glanced around, her apprehension sharpened. There were a couple of geraniums in one of the ferneries, and they looked vibrantly healthy. Could her father have arranged for someone to come in and water them? A neighbor perhaps—the same neighbor who had carelessly left the front door unlocked? That was the most probable explanation. She breathed a little easier and rejoined her son.

"What do you say we take our bags up to our room?"

"Okay!" Casey answered enthusiastically.

They went up to the room that Joanna had used as a teenager, a lovely room with a marvelous view of the ocean. It contained two single maple beds and two matching bureaus. A lavender flower-print paper covered the walls.

Joanna opened the windows and checked the bed linens. Then she gave her son a glance. He seemed thoroughly at ease. He'd dumped all his clothes onto the floor and was sorting them into the various drawers of "his" bureau.

Seeing that he was happily occupied, Joanna slipped out to the hall and peeked into her father and Viv's room. A shadow of apprehension still lingered in her heart. But the room appeared to be in perfect order.

She tiptoed down the hall to the room that had been Michael's. The door was closed. She touched the knob, then backed away at the sudden wrenching onslaught of memories.

But this behavior was all so silly, she chided herself. Michael no longer existed for her. Where was the uncaring, independent attitude she had lived with for six years? She closed her eyes, deliberately slowing her breath for a few moments.

She turned the knob and opened the door.

Suddenly every nerve in her body jerked as if an electric current were shooting through it. Her heart stopped beating altogether.

There, asleep on the bed, wearing nothing but a pair of cutoff jeans, was Michael Malone in the flesh.

CHAPTER TWO

"Michael!" Joanna shrieked.

He woke with a start, his dark head snapping up in alarm and confusion.

Her legs were so weak they buckled, and she clung to the door for support.

He bolted into a sitting position, his body instantly tensed and ready to spring. "What...? Who...? No...it's not—" His voice registered a shock that matched her own. He shot to his feet and rubbed his eyes. "Joanna?"

They stared at each other for what seemed an eternity, lips slightly parted as if they wanted to speak but couldn't find the words. This wasn't happening to her, Joanna thought. This had to be a dream. Any minute now she would wake up and find it was just her mind playing a trick, just a memory suddenly become too vivid.

"Joanna?" he repeated incredulously. "Is it really you?"

No, this was no dream. That voice . . . that face . . .

"Michael?" her thin voice quaked.

They had not run into each other once during the past six years. Neither had they talked on the phone or written. In all that time, not a single word of explanation had been exchanged between them, not one word to justify his cold betrayal of her after so intimate a summer. Not even a measly, "Gee, I'm sorry you got hurt, kid."

And as Joanna stared at Michael now, she realized those words could never be exchanged. It was far too late. The appropriate time was past, buried under years of leading separate lives.

"What are you doing here?" she cried tremulously, her pulse racing with emotions too confused to sort.

The sleep seemed to pass from his body even as she stared at him, and he suddenly looked at her with a clear, cool control. "What am *I* doing here? Oh, no, the question is, what are you doing here?"

"M-my father asked me to stay here and watch the house. He and V-Viv are on the West Coast this summer."

Michael's eyes narrowed. "Is that so? Well, for your information, my mother happened to invite me here for the very same reason." His eyes were still the same brilliant cobalt she used to admire so much, but something about them had changed. Now they harbored a coldness she wasn't used to, a cynicism...

"But that can't be!" she gasped. Did he think she had just taken a notion to barge in uninvited?

"The hell it can't!" He yanked a shirt from the back of a chair and whipped it on. "And since neither Jim nor she would be so insensitive as to invite the two of us here at the same time, one of us must be lying." He started to button the shirt, but oddly his fingers kept fumbling ineffectually and he finally gave up the effort.

"So it seems," she retorted, vaguely wondering why he should consider anyone who brought them together "insensitive." You'd think he was the one who'd been used and two-timed.

In the heavy silence that followed, Joanna studied his broad, rigid shoulders, the long, corded stretch of his legs. He'd grown heavier over the years, but all the weight was muscle. And if such a thing were possible, he'd become even more handsome. His face had taken on character. He seemed so mature. Not that his hair wasn't still the solid rich brown it had been six years ago; it was. And his body remained firm and lean. But there had been something almost coltish about the Michael she had known, something youthful. Now he was all man.

"Well?" she prodded.

"Well what, Joanna?" he snapped.

"What are we going to do about it?" she asked, making an effort to lift her chin.

"Well, I'd say we have a little problem on our hands, wouldn't you?"

"Then I suggest you leave."

Michael tossed back his dark head and laughed scornfully. "Not on your life! *You* leave."

"I will not! My father invited me here, I've been on the road since dawn, I'm exhausted, and I'm not budging!" She paused abruptly as a sudden thought struck her. She glanced around. "Where's Bunny?"

Michael's brow lowered in a thunderous scowl. "What!"

"I said, where's Bunny? I was just wondering if your wife was suddenly going to waltz in here and try to throw me out, too." She flicked back her long, pale gold hair, pretending the ice in his eyes wasn't disturbing her.

"You're not serious, are you?" he asked quietly.

"Serious? Why, yes. About what?" she said in confusion.

"Bunny. You're not trying to pretend you don't know?"

"Know what?"

"We're divorced!" His eyes flicked over her with palpable derision.

Joanna felt herself paling. "Divorced?"

Pinning her with a cold, incisive stare, Michael began to applaud, giving slow, loud claps. "Bravo, Joanna! A wonderful performance!"

His attitude quickly turned her shock into anger. The man was insufferable! How could she ever have loved him? "What are you talking about, Michael? This is the first news I've heard about any divorce of yours." Then a bit more hesitantly, "When did it happen?"

He glanced up at the ceiling in exasperation. "Joanna, I'm hardly in a conversational mood at the moment. This situation...you showing up out of the blue...*dammit*!" With that, he strode across the room and, being careful not to touch her, hurried out to the hall.

But within seconds, his footsteps came to a halt. "Joanna!"

"What!" she snapped, spinning herself out of the room.

Michael was standing by her room. From around the door, a pair of large, teary blue eyes was staring up at him.

She ran across the hall and knelt beside her son. Immediately he flung his arms around her neck and buried his face in her long hair. She glared up at Michael, feeling like an enraged lioness with her cub.

"Now see what you've done."

"Me? I ... How was I supposed to know?"

"Oh, just go away! Go away and leave us alone!" She rocked Casey in her arms, soothing him with a kiss.

"Is that your son?" His voice was hollow and flat, his eyes dark with unreadable emotion.

Joanna nodded and pried Casey's arms from around her neck. "It's all right, babe. No need to cry."

But the child nuzzled back and sobbed into her ear, "But you and that man were fighting, Ma. Make him go away."

Michael's mouth tightened and he thrust a hand through his hair. "Will you tell the kid I'm not going to hurt you?" he said with only the briefest of glances downward.

"The 'kid's' name is Casey, and you can tell him yourself!" Joanna hissed, hugging her son closer.

Slowly, reluctantly, Michael lowered himself to the floor. As his eyes narrowed on Casey, it occurred to Joanna that he had never been allowed the joy or sense of fulfillment that comes with being a parent. She also realized that Casey was the same age his and Bunny's child would have been.

"Don't be scared," he began. "My name is Michael. I ... I'm your uncle, sort of."

Casey peeked up from Joanna's shoulder. "My uncle? Mom's never told me about you."

Michael stared down at his long, graceful hands and smiled ruefully. "No, I don't suppose she has." After a thoughtful pause, "You know Vivien, don't you? The woman who's married to your grandfather?"

Casey nodded cautiously.

"Well, she's my mother."

"Oh." Casey stood up straighter. "I like Grandpa Scott and Viv. They took me for a ride up Mount Washington."

"Yes . . . well, I'm Viv's son," Michael repeated.

Lights began to go on behind Casey's eyes as he made the connections. "Do you live here, too?" he inquired, wiping his nose on the back of his arm.

"Yes, this summer anyway." Michael shot a quick glance at Joanna, daring her to refute him. In spite of the trembling that still racked her body, she managed to glare back with convincing contempt.

Casey nodded thoughtfully. Then, much to Joanna's dismay, his face broke into a smile of acceptance. "When do you have supper in this house?" he asked with his usual congeniality. "I'm starved. I had a hot dog on the boat, but a sea gull ate it."

Michael rose abruptly. Obviously he had no desire to get any closer to this child. Perhaps he even resented him.

"Don't bother Michael about supper, Casey. As soon as you've washed your face and hands, I'll take you out for a bite."

The child looked up uncertainly from one adult to the other.

"That's not necessary, Jo. There's food in the kitchen."

But Joanna looked away as if she couldn't stand the sight of him. "I'd rather starve first."

"Suit yourself." Disdain reentered his demeanor. "I just thought you might want to consider the boy first." He turned to leave. "But then, you never were the type to think of anyone but yourself. I guess it was stupid of me to expect you'd changed." He strode back into his room and slammed the door.

Joanna stared at the closed door in a maelstrom of confused emotion. What in heaven's name was he talking about?

Shakily she ushered her son into the bathroom and helped him wash. "Now, go back to the bedroom and change into a clean T-shirt. I want to freshen up, too. Then we'll go out to a restaurant, okay?''

Casey nodded, stumbling tiredly over his new, thick-soled sneakers.

Left to herself, Joanna gazed into the mirror over the sink. Her cheeks looked fevered. Her eyes were wild. She thought she might actually vomit. And to think, she'd come here to relax, find inner peace, give her life direction!

No wonder she had felt such deep misgivings on the ferry. She'd been concerned about bad memories—but now Michael himself was here. She should have listened to her intuition.

Joanna put a trembling hand to her heart. It was racing so fast she grew frightened. What was happening to her? And, why had she reacted to Michael that way? Such anger! Such contempt! She'd been like a stranger to herself, saying and feeling things that were totally foreign to her. Sure, Michael had hurt her, but that was a long time ago. She'd recovered from the pain and anger and moved on . . . hadn't she? Of course she had, she assured her pitiful reflection.

At that moment, she heard Michael's footsteps in the hall. She tensed, but he continued on down the stairs. At the bottom, he picked up the phone and began to dial. She looked up and was horrified to see how wild her eyes had turned again, just at the sound of his step.

She washed her face with cold water and patted it dry. The towel smelled disturbingly of a musky aftershave or perhaps a soap. Quickly she draped it back over the bar.

She supposed it was reasonable to think they could meet again, although she'd honestly come to believe they never would. After all, she had thought that he and Bunny lived in Virginia. What were the chances of their ever crossing paths, especially since Joanna never visited her father where Michael, by coincidence, might be visiting his mother? But who would have guessed they would meet here, at this particularly difficult time in her life?

She knew she hadn't handled the meeting well. Seeing him so unexpectedly had stripped her of all the defenses she'd constructed over the years. Anger had flared, emotion flowed too spontaneously—which still came as a shock to Joanna, who considered herself empty of emotion.

But that behavior had to end right now, she reprimanded her image in the mirror. She didn't know where the anger had come from, or why, but it was stupid and inappropriate, and it had to end. She didn't need any more problems. She had to return to a sense of calm, retreat behind her safe wall of pride and independence.

She gave her clothes a quick check in the full-length mirror. Her denim skirt and blue knit jersey were rumpled from the journey, but they would have to do. She didn't want to spend any more time here than she had to, not even to change. She needed to put a little distance between herself and Michael before she confronted him again. Perhaps after a meal she would feel better. Maybe then she'd even be able to discuss the cottage rationally.

She brushed her hair, which shimmered in a golden cascade of waves to midback, then applied a touch of lipstick and a dusting of blush. She didn't look all that bad considering how distraught she felt. Perhaps a bit too pale and thin, but time in the sun would cure the first malady, and as far as the second went, her recent loss of weight seemed finally to have carved cheekbones into her face. It had sculpted the womanly curves of her body, too, in a way that made them more obvious, alluring even.

For one treacherous moment, she wondered if Michael had noticed. Had he studied the changes in her the way she had studied them in him? She doubted it. While they'd been arguing, she'd had the feeling that he was completely immune to her as a physical being, totally disinterested and disenchanted in her as a female. Disenchanted? Why, the man had barely been able to contain his contempt.

But that didn't make any sense! What reason did he have to be so angry? Her showing up unexpectedly at the cottage? Now that he was single again, was he planning to use the place to make up for lost time? Had her arrival scuttled his plans?

Or... or was it guilt lying heavily on his heart? Did Michael Malone actually have a conscience?

No, she wouldn't let herself worry about it any further. Michael meant nothing to her. Less than nothing! And any sort of feeling, even loathing, was just so much wasted energy.

"Casey?" Joanna called, leaving the bathroom. "Casey, are you ready to leave?"

When she received no reply, she pushed open the door. Her son was sprawled across the bed, fast asleep. The child was obviously exhausted. At the moment he didn't need food. What he needed was sleep, and it had been self-centered of Joanna not to notice sooner. She'd been so hellbent on getting out of the house and away from Michael. She paused abruptly. Michael had called her self-centered, too, had said she thought of no one but herself. Was it possible? Had Michael noticed Casey's tiredness when she, his own mother, hadn't?

She tiptoed in and covered him with an afghan. Then she pulled down the shades and stood at the foot of the bed wondering what to do next. Michael was still downstairs; she could hear his angry pacing. She also knew she couldn't hide out in her room all night. And though she dreaded the very thought of it, she was going to have to face him once again.

CHAPTER THREE

JOANNA TOOK A DEEP BREATH and remembered her resolution to stay calm and civil. It was the only course to take. Becoming angry would only work against her. It might lead Michael to think she was still hurting from the pain he'd inflicted six years ago. Which, she reminded herself, she definitely was not. He might even, heaven forbid, get the notion he still had some control over her.

She found him in the kitchen, buttering a slice of pasty-looking white bread. He had changed into a pair of tan denims and a cream-colored shirt that revealed a shadow of dark chest hair beneath. He'd brushed his thick, curling hair into a semblance of neatness, too, yet he still exuded an air of just-bridled sensuality.

"You've changed your mind about going out?" he asked, letting his cool blue eyes graze hers briefly.

Joanna forced a smile. "How'd you guess?"

"I saw the kid asleep when I left my room."

Joanna ignored the resentment she felt over Michael's reference to Casey as "the kid." She replied with amazing equanimity, "I guess the trip was too much for him. He's out cold."

Michael looked thoroughly disinterested. "Do you want some of this?" He gestured toward a pot of glutinous canned soup on the stove.

"No. No, thanks."

"You should eat something." He tugged open a cupboard door. "Here, help yourself." His face seemed cast in stone. She couldn't tell what he was thinking. It was as if he, too, had had time to reflect on his reaction to her arrival and was regretting the harsh words. She grew uneasy at his solicitude.

"I called my mother a few minutes ago," he said, going back to stirring his soup.

"Oh?" Joanna turned with a can of beef stew in her hand.

Michael shuffled to the refrigerator and took out a bottle of wine. Wine and canned soup?

"I had to find out what was going on here—you know, both of us being invited to the cottage . . ."

"And?" Joanna prompted impatiently when he began to rummage through a drawer for a corkscrew.

"She apologized for the mix-up. It was simply a matter of crossed wires. Evidently she invited me to stay here, Jim invited you, and neither of them told the other what they'd done until it was too late and we'd both accepted."

Joanna stared at him dumbfoundedly. "Just like that? Crossed wires . . . and she's sorry?"

"That's what I said. But it was obviously an honest mistake. She'd flown out to my aunt's, and your father was busy in Boston. They didn't have a chance to check with each other." Michael's voice was suspiciously level and calm.

"It's a pretty lame excuse, if you ask me. Want to know what I think? I think my father deliberately didn't tell your mother he'd asked me here because he knew she wouldn't like the idea of my being here for the summer. In fact, I bet she didn't know that he'd invited me until you called." Michael suddenly made a great production out of opening the wine. "I'm right, aren't I?" When he failed to respond, Joanna turned and slipped the can into the automatic opener. "So what are we supposed to do now? Does she have a solution?"

"Sure. She suggested you go back where you came from."

Joanna sent what she hoped was a malevolent glance over her shoulder.

"And then Jim jumped in and suggested I find a motel. Then . . . well, I hung up in mid-argument."

"Great! So what now? I was planning to stay the whole summer."

"So was I." They stared at each other, locked in impasse.

"Well, I'm not leaving," she said a little too adamantly. "I've been telling Casey about this place for weeks. He'd be crushed if I suddenly told him we were going home. You can't imagine how he's been looking forward to this . . . all the toys he's packed to play in the sand . . . the list of souvenirs he wants to buy." She also remembered how much he needed to be here, away from all the people and places that constantly reminded him of Phil. The more she thought about it, the firmer she grew in her conviction. "I'm not leaving," she repeated.

"Well, I'm not, either," Michael shot back. "I'm not here just to get a suntan, kiddo. I have some very important work to do." He clunked the wine bottle down so hard some of its contents sloshed out. Immediately he seemed to regret his open display of tension and forced a quick, tight smile.

"I'm not here to get a suntan, either, kiddo," she mocked, forcing a smile as phony as the one he'd just dealt her.

"You could use one. You're as pale as a ghost. All skin and bones, too. Don't you ever eat?" His eyes traveled over her in a way that made her terribly self-conscious.

Suddenly she felt the strangest ùrge to throw the can—stew, opener, and all—right into his dark, cynical face. But she didn't. "Thank you," was all she said. "You always knew how to make me feel so wonderful." She scooped the stew into a pot and slung it onto a burner.

Joanna hated their standing so close. There seemed to be a field of electricity crackling between them. And when their arms brushed by accident, they both jerked away as if they'd just been burned.

Finally Michael broke the silence. "So, how have you been, Jo?" he asked with a heavily mocking slur.

"Terrific!" she spat. "Yourself?"

"Great!" he returned with waspish sarcasm.

She scraped her hasty meal into a bowl and lifted it off the counter. "So, you're great and I'm terrific, but that still doesn't solve our problem, does it?" With that, she pivoted on her heel and bolted for the dining room.

A minute later, Michael joined her, pushing a serving cart so recklessly the china and silverware on it nearly clattered off. Joanna glanced at the cart and then at her muddy stew. Neither of them was having what could be called a decent meal.

With quick, impatient moves, he set his bowl on the table, poured a glass of wine, and sat. But he didn't eat. He just stared at Joanna in brow-furrowed concentration. It was unnerving.

"A-aren't you going to eat?" she asked.

He didn't answer, just went on staring. Her eyes darted nervously around the room.

"Jo, listen. This sniping is getting us nowhere," he finally said in a conciliatory tone.

"I agree completely."

He sighed a long, thoughtful sigh. "So, how about if we share the cottage?"

Joanna dropped her spoon. "You can't be serious."

"Dammit, Jo! I don't know what else we can do. We both have legitimate reasons for being here, and neither of us intends to leave."

Alarm swept like fire through Joanna's nerves. "Impossible!"

"Why? We're both adults."

"And what's that supposed to mean?" That they were no longer the star-struck youngsters to whom sharing a house would have meant the world?

"It means we should be able to work out a daily routine that keeps us from getting in each other's hair. Of course,

he kid might be a complication we'll have to work on,
but—"

In spite of her resolution to remain civil, Joanna exploded. "My son has a name, you know! It won't kill you
to say it!"

"All right, Jo, back off," he snapped. "I didn't mean
anything by it."

"Like hell you didn't!"

The room vibrated with anger for a moment, then, like
dust settling, gradually went calm again. But Joanna was
now positive it was a shallow calm. Each of them was as
tense as a live wire with the effort to be amicable. And that
scared her.

Lord knew she'd had reason enough to be angry at him
six years ago. He had acted unconscionably toward her, the
way he'd played at love so convincingly, promising her the
sky, all the while knowing how inexperienced and impressionable she was. Unconscionable and heartless, leading
her in some kind of grotesque dance of the emotions when
all the while he was secretly seeing Bunny. The lies, the de-
ceptions cloaked in such sincerity, the lack of respect for
her—that was what got to her most. Yes, she'd been
crushed when she found out what Michael Malone was
really all about. She couldn't remember ever crying as hard
as she did that night. But when the sun rose she also discovered that she was angry. Furiously angry.

She supposed she was lucky to have found anger so
quickly. It had been a great defense, keeping her from falling apart altogether. But the pain and humiliation never
went away completely, either. They were always there, all
mixed up with the anger in a turbulent sea of emotional
confusion. But it was the anger that saved her. It kept her
from wallowing and got her walking, albeit resentfully, into
the future again.

But all that had passed. She couldn't have gone on living with such bitterness and pain. There was Phil and her
job, learning to cook and keep house—and then there was
Casey. So many good things to fill her life, to replace the

anger. Only now she wondered if her new life had really replaced the anger or merely covered it over. Did unresolved feelings really ever disappear just because a person wanted them to? Or did they lie in the shadows of one's personality, ominously ticking away...?

She took a spoonful of stew, which turned to sawdust in her mouth. In cold silence, Michael picked up his bread and ripped off a bite.

"I think I'm going to live to regret this," she murmured grudgingly, "but all right, we'll share."

Michael stopped chewing and something strange and unreadable flickered across his expression.

"But I'll buy my own groceries," she went on quickly, "of which I already owe you a can of—"

"Forget it."

"No way. I don't want to owe you anything." She noticed one dark eyebrow arch. "As I was saying, I'll handle all my meals, you can handle yours. That goes for laundry and cleaning, too. In other words, I'll go my way, you go yours. Understand?"

"Perfectly. And as I was saying before I was so graciously interrupted, I'd appreciate it if you'd keep the...your son from being disruptive while I'm working, especially in the morning."

"Casey is never disruptive! He's the most well-behaved child you'll ever meet!"

"But he *is* a child." Michael's tone presumed to end the argument.

"You needn't worry. I'll keep him as far away from you as humanly possible."

The corner of Michael's mouth lifted fractionally. "Good. Then we shouldn't have any problems."

"Let's hope not." Joanna picked up her bowl, lifted her chin and retreated to the kitchen.

There, after hastily rinsing off her dishes, she collapsed onto a chair and lowered her face into her hands. An uncontrollable shaking racked her body. It had happened again. In spite of all her coolly reasoned intentions, Michael had still been able to make her blood boil. She didn't understand it. She harbored no grudges against Michael for the past; she suffered no recriminations.

Joanna dropped her hands limply into her lap and sighed defeatedly. Of course she begrudged Michael. In fact, at this moment she hated him! And if she begrudged him and hated him, it could only mean she was still carrying around all the other emotional baggage as well. The loss and regret; the pain and humiliation, too. She had thought she was over all that. She'd thought she was free. But obviously, she wasn't.

This was incredible, so unfairly incredible! After six careful years, how could Michael be back in her life? He'd stopped existing for her, or so she had thought. How could he be sitting in the very next room?

Oh, why did Phil have to die? She should be home with him now, lingering over dinner, quietly talking about their day at the shop. *Share?* Had she actually agreed to share the cottage with Michael? Was she out of her mind?

No! She wouldn't let herself get all worked up. Michael wasn't worth it. She had contained the anger and pain once before, when it was fresh and far more searing. She could do it again, she was sure. Besides, she refused to let Michael see that he could still upset her. Where was her pride?

She took a few calming breaths and got to her feet. By the time she was on her way back through the dining room, she had regained her composure.

"Not going to bed already, are you?" he asked, still sitting at the table.

She turned slowly from the stairs. "Sure. Why not?"

"It's not even eight o'clock yet. Besides, we've hardly talked." She hesitated. "Come on," he laughed. "I won't bite."

Joanna moved to the table reluctantly.

"How about a glass of wine? You didn't have anything to drink with your supper."

"And you didn't have anything to eat with yours."

Michael grinned and pushed his untouched soup aside. Then he reached into the liquor cabinet for a glass. He poured it half-full and slid it to her side of the table, then refilled his own.

"So, how have you been, Joanna?"

"You asked me that already."

"Yes, I know. But I don't think your answer was very honest. This year must have been pretty rough on you."

"Are you referring to my husband's death?" she asked coolly though her hand shook as she lifted the wine to her lips.

"Uh huh."

She studied his face and saw nothing—no compassion, no curiosity, not even satisfaction that she had suffered. The man was as emotionless as stone. That, or he had become used to masking his feelings, too. Well, two could play at that game. "Yes, Phil's death was rough, but it wasn't as if I didn't know what was coming."

"Leukemia, wasn't it?"

For a moment, Joanna's expression crumbled and a sorrow she thought she'd overcome filled her heart. "Yes."

"Are you managing all right?"

She stared into the cold blue eyes across from her and her pride rekindled. "Very well. Phil was young, but he was very responsible. He left us with no bills, a roof over our heads, and...and enough savings to get us through life without too many problems." Joanna had all she could do to keep the shock she was suddenly feeling from registering in her expression. Why was she lying to him? Where had that statement come from?

Michael stared back, a man who once had known her better than she knew herself, yet he seemed totally unaware of her deceit. "Sounds like you're doing okay financially, but what about, you know, socially, emotionally?"

Joanna couldn't figure out what he was getting at. Did he want her to say she was desperately lonely and unable to function? "Well, I'm usually too busy to worry about so-cial or emotional problems, which probably means I don't have any to begin with. I'm the—the manager of a clothing store in North Conway." She had almost claimed to be its owner. "It's a nice little place, very trendy, yet not so upscale that the locals won't come in." She took a long sip from her glass.

Michael's eyes narrowed and she looked away, afraid her own eyes might betray her. She knew it didn't make sense, but she would be damned before she'd let Michael know that she'd been anything but perfectly happy after *he* had dropped out of her life. Phil's illness had been long and emotionally wrenching; his funeral had wrung her out. Litigation over confused property settlements had embattled her for months. Then there had been the loneliness and fear, the financial problems and the worrisome changes in Casey. She could tell Mr. Malone a lot he didn't suspect about her life. But she would *not*!

"How's Casey taking his father's death?"

"He's doing very well. He's a resilient child. But, naturally, he still misses Phil at times. They were very close." She sipped her wine and gazed boldly at the stone face across from her. "Phil was a wonderful father, right from the start, always there to change a diaper or sit up with Casey when he had a cold." She was amazed at the amount of satisfaction she derived from bragging. It was sort of like thrusting small, cold knives into Michael's heart, satisfying a strange, deep-seated need in her for—for what? Revenge? She didn't really understand it, but the longer she and Michael talked the more she felt like...like hitting him!

"He must have been a great help to you," he commented with cloying politeness.

"Yes, he was. But enough about me. What have you been up to? Are you still teaching down in Virginia?"

She watched his brow lower, his thoughts racing behind his eyes. "No...yes. What I mean is, I'm taking a leave of absence this year."

"Oh? Tired of teaching so soon?" she asked with a perverse desire to have him admit he wasn't as happy or as brilliant as Vivien had always implied.

"Not at all. I've loved every minute of it," he asserted, taking a huge swig of wine. "I've been very lucky, too—the right place at the right time. Just as I was finishing the dissertation for my Ph.D, the head of the Literature Department retired and I was offered his position."

"You're head of the department? And...and you have your doctorate?" Joanna sipped her wine slowly, thoughtfully. Strangely a part of her wanted to congratulate him, but another part held her back. Instead, she looked up with a sardonic little smile. "How prestigious! *Dr.* Malone! Bunny must have loved that." There was a moment of silence. She could almost hear ice crystalizing in the air between them.

"Yes, she was very proud of me. But she especially loved all the entertaining we did because of my position. The president of the college said she was the best hostess the faculty ever had."

Joanna was sorry she'd introduced Bunny into the conversation. Now her beautiful image was etched into all the shadows of the darkening room. She would have fit so well into that milieu, too, coming as she did from a home where so much entertaining had gone on.

"Do you mind if I ask why you two got a divorce?"

Michael hesitated, his brow creased. "We were both deeply upset by the separation, but it was a mutual decision agreed on only after months of agonized discussion. You see, Bunny is a very talented person. She studied fashion design in college and wanted to pursue a career of her own. Naturally she wanted to move to New York to be at the center of the industry, but that was impossible for me because of my job. I finally realized I had no right to hold her back, and she didn't want to hinder me, either, so..." He raised his eyebrows with a sad, resigned look.

"Oh, so it was a career choice that split you up?"

"Yes, that alone."

Joanna studied him carefully over the rim of her glass. There was no reason to doubt him, and yet there was something about his voice she didn't trust, a bravado that matched her own a little too closely.

"I guess things worked out for you in the long run then— the fact that you had no children, I mean."

"Oh, I don't know. I miss not having children. We were really looking forward to the baby she miscarried." His eyes were now so hooded he seemed to have withdrawn into a deep, dark cave within himself.

"I know what you mean," Joanna commiserated. Her head was beginning to feel like a balloon. "A child can bring so much pleasure to a marriage, bring two people really close."

"Yes, I can imagine. It . . . it would have been a boy."

"You knew?" She watched him refill their glasses.

"Uh huh. They told us at the hospital. We'd planned on calling him . . . uh, Peter. After his Grandfather Wilcox."

Joanna digested this bit of information slowly. Then, perhaps because of the unrelieved tension, the fixed smile on her face began to quiver. For a moment, she was afraid she was going to laugh right out loud.

"What's the matter?" Michael emerged from the deep privacy of his thoughts, and was suddenly defensive.

"Oh, nothing. But with a mother named Bunny, could you have named him anything else?" She gulped down a huge mouthful of wine to cover the irreverently giddy leap her voice had taken. And if they'd had other children, she wondered, would they have named them Flopsy, Mopsy, and Cottontail?

Remorse gripped her almost immediately. How could she be so cruel, finding humor in someone else's tragedy?

Michael shifted his weight as if he were sitting in a nest of burrs. "Speaking of which, your son has an interesting name. How did you come up with the name Casey?"

"M-my son?" Joanna's spine straightened as a shaft of emotion shot through her from an unexpected angle. Though she didn't understand it, the air around her now seemed to bristle with vague, undefinable danger. Suddenly she felt defensive toward Casey. Protective.

"Phil and I took a trip down to Florida right after we were married. We went on AmTrak and, to the best of my knowledge, our son was conceived on the journey down."

"Oh, I see," Michael murmured darkly. "Casey. Trains. I see."

It was a total fabrication. Joanna had simply been fond of the name. She sat back, shocked at having caught herself lying again. But the words had spilled out so instinctively. For one unfathomable moment she had been gripped by fear, and without any forethought, that story had tumbled out. She wasn't controlling this game of duplicity anymore. Some other force was doing the controlling for her. She had to prove that Michael had not hurt her, that she had survived him and even thrived. She wanted to rub his smug face in the fact that she had been happy, that her marriage had been perfect. She knew it had a lot to do with her strong sense of personal pride. *That* she could understand. But it also seemed to be yoked to something else, a disturbing, indistinct fear of what might happen if Michael found out that she'd lied. And *this* she didn't understand.

Michael stared out into the darkening night beyond Joanna. His face was like granite.

Are you simmering, you unconscionable, two-timing louse? she thought. *Are you remembering how much I loved you? Are you thinking it could have been us on that train? Are you sorry you missed out on the life I could have given you?*

But when he focused on her again, his eyes told her he didn't give the slightest damn. She meant nothing to him—just as she'd always suspected. For all he was affected, they could have been two strangers making idle conversation on a bus.

"Bunny and I went to Florida, too, a couple of times. It's a wonderful place, but nothing beats Jamaica. That's where we went on our honeymoon. Jamaica's incredible in October.''

A montage of images flashed through Joanna's mind—Michael and Bunny running through a tropical surf, Michael and Bunny sharing an intimate dinner at a luxury hotel, Michael and Bunny making love! And all just weeks—weeks!—after they themselves had talked of getting married.

Suddenly Joanna didn't want to continue this game. It was getting out of hand. If she continued, she suspected she would come out of it the loser. She usually had whenever she'd tangled with Michael. She rose abruptly.

"Well, if you don't mind, I'm ready to call it a night. I'm really bushed.'' She yawned. "And Casey's an early riser. But I'm glad we took this time to talk. It's been . . . really nice.''

Michael's glacier-blue eyes stabbed her with sudden mockery. "Sure. It's been a ball.''

"Good night'' was all she said. She even managed a smile.

He laughed softly, leaning back in his chair like a dark, avenging devil. "Sweet dreams, Joanna.''

She hurried up the stairs, but even before she reached her room, tears of frustration were clouding her vision.

CHAPTER FOUR

AT THE OUTER MARGINS of Joanna's consciousness, there was a soft, rapid tapping. Rain hitting the windows of her New Hampshire home. But when she opened her eyes, sunlight was fanning around the edges of the window shades, washing unfamiliar furniture with pale, impressionistic light. On a swift wave of sickening awareness, she remembered where she was.

Again the tapping. She lay very still and listened harder. It was coming from across the hall—from Michael's room—from a typewriter. He had mentioned he was doing some work here at the cottage this summer, though he hadn't explained exactly what it was. Work toward another degree perhaps? An article for a professional journal? Joanna yawned and pushed the question out of her mind. She really didn't care what Michael Malone was doing!

In spite of the fact that she'd been exhausted the previous night, it had taken her hours to fall asleep. She had listened to house sounds—Michael's footsteps pacing through the rooms downstairs, the occasional burble of the propane tank below her window, Casey's soft breathing in the adjacent bed. Around eleven she had heard Michael leave. Where he went, she had no idea. All she knew was that sleep eluded her until he came in hours later. And during that time she'd kept thinking about everything they'd said—and everything they hadn't. Especially that. It was so ironic. She felt sure that their last summer together was as much on his mind as it was on hers; it had to be. Yet neither of them had dared broach the subject, as if they refused to acknowledge it had ever happened. Ah, well. Probably all for the best. No, definitely for the best. She really preferred to ignore that time in her life. She had enough problems these days and she certainly didn't need to compound them by dwelling on the past.

She pushed back the long veil of her hair and glanced at the clock. Good heavens! It was already quarter to nine! Casey usually woke up around seven.

She spun around. His bed was empty and toys were strewn on the floor. But he was nowhere in sight. Joanna jumped out of bed and not bothering with robe or slippers, went running out to the hall and down the stairs.

"Casey?" she called, trying not to panic. "Casey, where are you?" She would never forgive herself if he had wandered off and hurt himself while she was sleeping. At the edge of the backyard, a wooden stairway led down the bluff to the pond, and at the bottom there was a dock where a few neighbors moored their boats. What could be a more alluring spot for a curious five-year-old—or a more dangerous one if he couldn't swim?

She raced out the back door, heart pounding furiously, then came to a sudden halt. In a nook of the yard, where the scruffy lawn gave way to sand and honeysuckle, Casey knelt playing with his cars and trucks. Joanna walked over and knelt beside him.

"Casey, you had me scared to death. I didn't realize you'd left the bedroom. Why didn't you wake me?"

The child shrugged. He was still dressed in pajamas. "Brrrm!" He pushed a miniature tow truck up a hill of sand.

"Well, next time I oversleep, wake me, okay?" He nodded. "Which reminds me, don't ever, ever wander out of this yard alone, you hear?"

"Uh huh." He looked up with a cherubic smile, and Joanna couldn't help hugging him and kissing his smooth cheek.

"Poor lamb, you must be starved, skipping supper last night and all."

"I had two cookies."

"Cookies! For breakfast?" She groaned and glared up at the house to a second-floor window. The curtain swung as if someone had just let it drop. She didn't expect Michael to feed her son, but at least he could have wakened her.

"Listen, I'm going to make us a nice big breakfast. You can stay here and play if you like. I'll call you in about fifteen minutes."

As soon as she and Casey had eaten, they packed a picnic lunch and set out for the beach, leaving the house all to Michael. It was a perfect day, sparklingly sunny and hot. They drove out to Katama Point.

Casey had never been to an ocean beach before and at first found the surf intimidating. But he soon got used to it and was dunking and splashing as if he had lived on the island all his life. He and Joanna built castles from the fine white sand, searched for pretty rocks and shells, and after lunch went swimming again.

By midafternoon, however, they'd had enough. Not only was the sun too strong, but without companions his own age, Casey had exhausted the beach's possibilities.

But Joanna wasn't ready to return to the cottage just yet. The air bristled there; emotions ran too high in spite of her efforts to keep them in tow. Feeling rather like a fugitive, she drove Casey to Oak Bluffs.

At the turn of the century it had been an elegant resort town. Now, crammed with souvenir shops and fast-food joints, the elegance had faded. Yet, Joanna loved Oak Bluffs. She loved the tiny cottages that lined the winding streets, with their gingerbread trim and Gothic windows, their tiny balconies and flowers spilling out of window boxes. Even Casey was fascinated by the dollhouse image these cottages presented.

But his eyes really lit up when Joanna led him to the attraction that had been her destination all along—The Flying Horses, a gaily painted carousel, one of the oldest in the country.

When Casey was securely buckled onto one of the horses, Joanna hopped onto one herself. Together, they rode until the music ended. Then they rode again, around and around, in never-ending circles.

Joanna could hear her son's shy laughter and was glad he was having a good time. But as for herself, she was growing unaccountably sad. The pain of losing Phil had lessened remarkably over the past couple of months. But there were still times when it came back for no reason. Was that what this sadness was all about now? For some reason she didn't think so. No, it had something to do with this place...this carousel. Michael had brought her here for the first time when she was sixteen and full of resentment.... And yet the feeling was like a feeling of grief for something lost.... And it was here the following year that Michael, half hanging off one of the horses, had recited a Byron poem to her—She Walks in Beauty—one line for each spin past the spot where she stood laughing.... Grief, then, for someone gone... And here that Michael had lifted her onto a horse the final summer and with knightly tenderness kissed her fingertips before handing her the reins. Suddenly Joanna realized her eyes were misting over as they rode around and around, going nowhere.

She was relieved when the ride finally ended. She and Casey walked down to the waterfront and found a restaurant with tables on an outdoor deck. They ordered delicious-looking hamburgers and fries, but knowing she would eventually have to return to the house and face Michael again robbed her of her appetite. She lowered her head and massaged her throbbing temples. This arrangement wasn't going to work. She'd been out of her mind thinking it would.

"Joanna? Joanna Scott?"

Joanna glanced up, responding unthinkingly to her maiden name. Walking toward her was a buxom, freckle-faced redhead in her mid-twenties.

"Meg?"

The girl nodded and laughed. "Good Lord, it *is* you! I thought I was seeing things. How are you, Jo?" Meg was a native islander whose family lived along the same pond as the Scotts. She was unquestionably one of Joanna's pleasanter memories of summers past.

"Okay. Yourself?"

"Great! But what are you doing here?"

"I'm staying at my father's. He and Viv are in California for the summer."

"That's terrific!" Her face beamed merrily while her red hair, as ebullient as her personality, puffed around it in a cloud of curls. "Oh, Jo, is this your little boy?"

Joanna nodded proudly. "Uh huh. Casey, this is an old friend of mine, Meggy Trent."

"McGonigle's the name now, Jo—has been for five years. Oh, he's adorable. Hi, Casey," she greeted, bending over. He gave her a ketchupy grin. "You look just about the age of my little boy, Paul. Are you four?"

Casey shook his head. "Five!"

"Oh, my! A much older man!"

"Meg, I didn't even know you were married. And you have a four-year-old son?"

"Yup. And a three-year-old son. And a nine-month-old daughter." Joanna couldn't help laughing at Meg's expression of mock exhaustion. "Do you remember Steve McGonigle? That's who I married. He and I were already dating the summer you and Mi..." Her words thinned to a whisper and her already florid complexion flushed.

"No, sorry, I don't remember him," Joanna intervened quickly. "Do you still live here?"

"Uh huh. Steve and I bought the house right next door to my parents'. It works out great for baby-sitting." She let her gaze wander over the boat-specked horizon a moment. Her face became pensive. "Mind if I sit awhile?"

"Please do."

"I won't be long. I'm just waiting for my brother, Nathan." Her head inclined toward a shop near the restaurant. "That's his place. He has another over in Edgartown.

He was just closing when a customer showed up. You remember Nathan, don't you?"

"Of course." Joanna smiled.

"Thought you would. He was nuts about you when we were kids." She paused and laughed. "You wouldn't give him the time of day, though, as I recall." Their eyes met briefly. "So, have you heard from Michael lately?"

"Believe it or not, I saw him yesterday for the first time in years. It turns out that he's planning to spend this summer at the cottage, too."

Meg's expression shifted with speculation, but, to Joanna's undying relief, she made no comment. "Jo, I heard you became a widow recently. It was last winter, wasn't it?"

"Yes, November." Joanna screwed her attention on a swirl of spilled salt and ran a pattern through it with her finger.

"I feel so bad for you. It was a tough break," Meg whispered.

Joanna shrugged, managing a wan smile. "Every day's a little easier."

"I hope I'm not prying, but what did he die of?"

"Leukemia."

Meg shook her head and made small, sad clicking noises with her tongue. "Then it wasn't a sudden thing, an accident or anything like that?"

"No, he was in and out of the hospital more than half the time we were married."

Meg reached over and squeezed Joanna's hand, her eyes filled with compassion. "Do you still live in New Hampshire?"

"Uh huh."

"And are you working?"

Joanna hated talking about her life. She wished Meg wouldn't ask. Nothing about it seemed right. Since Phil's death, it was all fragments running in purposeless directions.

Just at that moment, Meg began to wave and spared her the agony of answering. "Over here. Nathan!"

Joanna's gaze followed Meg's with a mild sense of anticipation.

"And you complain about the way I talk," he said, grinning. He gave Joanna a cursory glance then immediately did a double take. "Joanna! What...?"

She couldn't help laughing at his surprise. "How are you, Nathan?"

"As of this moment, terrific!" He was a handsome man, though short and slightly stocky. He had thick red-brown hair, a shade darker than his neatly trimmed beard, warm brown eyes and a sensitive mouth. It all added up to an engaging appearance that somehow reminded Joanna of a cuddly teddy bear.

"What are you doing here?" he asked.

"She's come to spend the summer," his sister cut in excitedly. "She's staying at her father's."

"Great!"

"I take it you're still living on the island?" Joanna asked.

"Oh, sure. In fact, I just finished building myself a new house."

"If you haven't already guessed, my brother's doing pretty well for himself."

"Sure looks that way. Meg told me you own a couple of shops...."

"Yes. Clothing stores."

"Really? I work in a clothing store back home."

"Well, well. Small world." His eyes sparkled warmly.

"And is there a Mrs. Trent these days?"

"Nah!" He paused and looked down at Casey. "I used to know somebody I thought I could settle down with, but evidently somebody else beat me to her."

Joanna laughed with a dismissive wave of her hand. "Nathan, this is my son, Casey. Casey, another old friend, Nathan Trent."

The child swallowed the last of his food and held out a hand. "Hi. Nice to meet you, sir."

Nathan's eyes crinkled. "Nice to meet you, too, Casey."

"Well, Nate, what do you say we hit the road," Meg suggested. "We're disturbing Joanna's meal. Besides, you still have to get over to the other shop to see how the new girl did today."

"Uh . . . right."

Meg rose. "Jo, it was really good seeing you again. We'll have to get together soon. And if you ever need a baby-sitter, don't hesitate to call. I'm home almost all the time, and if I'm not available I have a list of sitters we can share."

"Thank you."

"I mean it."

Joanna laughed. "I believe you do."

"Well, so long." Nathan waved and gave Joanna one last incredulous look. "Bye, Casey."

The next minute they were gone, and the smile they had brought to Joanna's face began to crumble. She could put off returning to the house no longer.

The sun was riding low when they arrived. It splashed gold across the pond, into the high leaves of the trees, over the silver-gray shingles of the commodious old house. Joanna showed Casey the outdoor shower her father had rigged up on the side of the house, and together they screamed and giggled as the cold downpour hit their backs.

"There, that ought to get the sand off us," Joanna said, still laughing.

Michael was at the small kitchen table when they came through the door, their wet hair plastered to their heads, towels wrapped tightly around their shivering bodies. He was hunched over a half-eaten TV dinner and a copy of *The New Yorker*. He looked tired and his eyes were red.

"Hey, Uncle Michael," Casey called through chattering teeth. "We went to the beach today."

"That so?" Michael continued reading.

"I went into the ocean," the child continued, nonetheless, pronouncing the word "ocean" in three distinct syllables.

Michael finally looked up, drawn by the boy's charming speech pattern. Joanna grew uneasy. Alone, she knew she could avoid Michael pretty well, but Casey was another matter. He could be such an open, friendly child, he was bound to get in Michael's way eventually, and she feared the encounter wouldn't be a pleasant one. Michael had made it clear that he did not want Casey underfoot.

"We don't have an ocean where we live," Casey continued, his blue eyes gleaming with excitement, undaunted by Michael's disinterest.

"And is that the first time you went swimming?"

"Yes, in the o-ce-an," Casey stated, small teeth chattering. His hair stuck up in dark, wet points all over his head. "We have a river near our house. I been swimming there plenty of times. You gotta be tough to swim there, though."

Michael put down his magazine with a slight huff. "Oh? And why's that?"

"'Cause it's so cold. My dad says the water comes from the top of the mountain, from the snow."

Michael shot Joanna a swift, inquiring glance at Casey's use of the present tense when referring to Phil.

"Let's go, Casey," Joanna said quickly. "Michael is trying to have his dinner. I'm afraid we're disturbing him."

"See you later, Uncle Michael," the boy called sweetly.

"So long, kid." His eyes were already back on the magazine.

On the way up the stairs, Joanna paused. "I wish you wouldn't call him *Uncle* Michael, Casey. He isn't really your uncle."

The child looked up, confused. "What is he then?"

"He's . . ." Joanna's heart suddenly seemed to turn into a hard ball of fire. "Nothing. Nothing, babe. Hey, come on. Let's go find a good ol' Dr. Seuss to read before bed."

The day was just a glimmer of lavender on the horizon when she again descended the stairs. She'd had trouble getting Casey settled. But after three stories and a glass of warm milk, he had finally fallen asleep.

Joanna had showered and was now ready to relax with a good magazine. It really hadn't been such a bad day after all, probably because she'd been away from the house—and Michael—for most of it.

She padded out to the darkened sun porch in bare feet and a green silk kimono and stood at the screen door watching the lights from other houses shimmer across the pond. She had no idea she had company until Michael cleared his throat. She jumped. Immediately her heart was pounding crazily.

He was slouched in one of the old wicker chairs at the far end of the porch, his feet propped up on the windowsill. His long fingers were casually linked around the base of a wineglass resting on his belt. He was looking at her intently, a soft breeze ruffling the dark hair over his forehead. Somewhere in the night, a foghorn sounded.

"The kid settled for the night?"

Poor Casey! Michael had evidently taken a real dislike to him.

"Yesss." She turned her gaze back to the pond, her hair swinging silkily over one shoulder and down her breast.

"It took long enough," Michael murmured. "Why do you pamper him so much? Why not just put him to bed and say good-night?"

Joanna's head swiveled around. "And why don't you mind your own business?" Immediately she was kicking herself for rising to his bait.

"Don't get all huffy again," he said with infuriating calm. "I was just asking a question."

"Well, I'd appreciate it if you'd keep questions like that to yourself."

"Fine. I go my way, you go yours. I remember."

"Right. Which reminds me, I used more of your food this morning. But don't worry, I'm keeping a careful list. I'll replace everything as soon as I get to a market."

"Fine." He continued to stare, his eyes cutting her with the intensity of a hot laser.

Joanna felt extremely uneasy, full of emotion, yet at a loss for words.

Suddenly the telephone rang.

"Ahh, saved by the bell!" Michael droned sardonically.

Joanna hurried into the dining room. "Hello?"

"Hi, Joanna? Nathan."

"Oh, hi. How are you?" She switched on the table lamp.

"Not bad, except for feeling rather like a jerk."

"Oh? And what brought that on?"

He sighed heavily. "Well, this afternoon when I bumped into you—Jo, I completely forgot to extend my condolences to you. I heard about your husband's death last winter, but it slipped my mind completely. I guess I was just so surprised to see you I couldn't think of anything else."

"Oh, for heaven's sake, Nathan! The thought never even crossed my mind."

"Still, I wish I'd said something. I hope you won't hold it against me."

"Of course not!" She looked up and saw Michael's dark, muscular form leaning against the doorjamb.

"I hope you mean it," Nathan continued, "because I want to ask you something. Since it's been quite a while since your husband's death, I thought perhaps...have you started going out socially yet?"

Joanna's nerves suddenly pulled tight. "With men?"

Nathan laughed his deep, hearty laugh. "No, with Martians."

She laughed, too, uneasily because Michael was watching so intently. "Not really."

"Well, how does the thought strike you now?"

"It's a little frightening. The thought of dating again, when I already feel so old and matronly—it isn't just frightening, it's positively ludicrous."

A muscle in Michael's jaw tightened, and she shot him an irritated glance.

"You, old and matronly? Never! All kidding aside, would you care to go out some time?"

Joanna ran a hand over the banister, staring at her ringless third finger. She had finally put away her wedding band in April, but so far she hadn't found any incentive to start stepping out. Perhaps Nathan was just what she needed. With a leap of courage, she said, "Sure, I'd love to."

Michael retreated into the shadows of the porch.

"If it'll make things easier for you, I can get my sister and brother-in-law to come along."

Joanna's breath trembled with relief. "That would be great. When?"

"Tomorrow night? Or is that too soon?"

"No, tomorrow's fine."

"Good, I'll be by around seven then."

Joanna hung up the phone in something of a daze and wandered back out to the sun porch. Michael was standing at the far end, scowling like thunder.

"Well, that certainly was an unexpected call." She was smiling, proud of the step she'd taken.

"You have a date tomorrow night?"

"Yes, with Nathan Trent. Remember him?"

Michael's laughter was a low, mirthless rumble from the shadows. "Yeah, I remember him. Boy, you don't waste much time."

Joanna bristled with offense. "I don't recall asking for your opinion."

"You're right." He raised a hand in concession. "But can I ask just one more question? What are you going to do about your son?"

Joanna dropped into a wicker chair, casually draping the silky green folds of her robe around her legs. "Hire a baby-sitter, of course."

"And where are you going to get a baby-sitter on such short notice? You don't even know anybody here."

Joanna felt her breath coming short. Still, she managed to smile. "I have connections."

Michael looked at her narrowly. "Good. I was afraid that because I'd agreed to share this place with you, you were beginning to assume you had a built-in baby-sitter."

"What?" Joanna stared across the room for a few stunned seconds. "Michael, let's get one thing straight right now. I don't want anything from you, not a single thing."

Michael glared down the straight line of his nose at her, eyes cold and fierce. "And evidently you never did." With that, he strode out of the room.

Joanna felt weak with reaction. Her head fell forward into her hands and she closed her eyes. From the dining room, there came the sound of dialing. There was a pause, and then Michael dialed again.

"Operator," she heard him say impatiently, "there's some trouble with my line. I'm trying to reach a number in New York but the line keeps going dead. Could you ring it for me, please?"

Joanna didn't want to eavesdrop, but . . .

"Hi, Joyce? Michael . . ."

Joanna opened her eyes. Her back straightened. But of course. Michael was single again and undoubtedly as footloose as ever.

"How was your flight? I was a little worried when you decided to go back on that private plane. Next time, take the regular shuttle. It's a lot more reliable than . . ." His words became muffled, and Joanna found herself rising from her seat to get closer to the doorway.

When she picked up the conversation again, he was discussing something about a plumber. Evidently the woman he was talking to had a cottage on the Vineyard and wanted him to call a plumber to fix a leaky faucet. Who was this Joyce anyway? The familiarity in his voice as he spoke to her produced a sudden unexpected uneasiness.

Joanna reprimanded herself for cowering in the shadows. After all, Michael had listened without compunction to her phone conversation. She strolled into the dining room with a nonchalance she hardly felt and started searching through the collection of old records in the stereo cabinet.

"Yes, that's all I called about," he continued, his voice deep and lingeringly sexy. "And to say thanks for last night." He laughed quietly at something the woman said.

Last night? Was that where he'd been till three in the morning?

"See you next weekend, Joyce."

Joanna threw a scratched copy of Tchaikovsky's *1812 Overture* onto the stereo and jerked on the switch, and only the fact that Casey was asleep upstairs kept her from turning the volume up full blast.

CHAPTER FIVE

AFTER ANOTHER RESTLESS NIGHT, Joanna dragged herself out of bed, wondering how her nerves would hold up to the tension of yet another day. Of course, she had shopping to do this morning, and this evening she would be out with Nathan. Now, if only she could do something about the rest of her time, the time she was forced to spend at the house with Michael.

She slipped into her favorite shopping dress, a teal-blue, cotton-knit shift with small cap sleeves and a belt that nipped in her waist. She brushed her hair up into a loose topknot and applied a little lipstick. Fortunately she hadn't burned as badly as she'd thought the day before. Her skin had merely taken on a red-gold tone that was actually rather attractive.

By eight o'clock, when Michael came down to the kitchen, she had the washer whirring, and she and Casey were digging into a hearty breakfast of pancakes and sausages.

"Morning," he greeted coolly from the doorway.

She turned. "There's coffee made." She had decided to try treating him as she would any other housemate, someone who deserved at least common courtesy.

One dark eyebrow lifted questioningly.

"Owe me," she replied with a small smile of concession.

He looked a little surprised. "Seems like it's going to be another nice day." He walked into the room and stared out one of the sunny windows.

"The radio says it'll be in the eighties." Joanna sipped her coffee and gazed at his profile, feeling a sudden, almost palpable awareness of his presence. He was still the most attractive man she had ever met—thick, dark hair looking as if some woman had just run her fingers through it, the mouth with the slightly debauched droop at the corners, the body that moved with the slow easy grace of one assured of his virility.

And it dismayed her that after all he'd done she could still see him this way. Not that those good looks actually affected her emotionally or physically, she reminded herself. Oh, no! She was definitely over that! It was just that she had never met anyone more handsome, and she wished she wasn't quite so aware of the fact, as objective as that fact was.

"So what are your plans for the day?"

"Grocery shopping. Laundry. The beach maybe. Yours?"

He said something about having to go into town, too...and seeing to a repair at a friend's cottage. But somehow, as he talked, Joanna lost track of his words and found herself watching the play of morning sun on his dark hair instead, the slant of it across his broad chest...

It was so odd, she thought. Once this man had been the soul and substance of her life. Once they'd been desperate to spend every minute in each other's arms. And now all they could talk about was the weather.

Well, perhaps that was best. She couldn't bear talking to him about anything more serious. Last evening's conversation had left her in a bad mood, all bottled up and wanting to scream for reasons she couldn't fathom.

Thank goodness for Casey. In his innocence, he filled the void with his chatter, giving the household an appearance of harmony.

Michael was scrambling a few eggs, and Casey, contentedly fed, was dredging out the clothes from the washer when Joanna went to the phone.

A few minutes later, it was all settled. She'd got the number of a local girl from Meg, called and arranged to have her come and stay with Casey that night. Not only that, Meg had insisted Joanna bring Casey over to play with her children instead of taking him to the market.

Pleased with her efficiency so early in the morning, she returned to the kitchen smiling. But at the door, she realized that while she'd been on the phone, Casey had finished his chore and gone out to the porch for his sand pail. Now he had the middle of the kitchen floor strewn with the seashells and rocks he'd collected at the beach the previous day and was chatting excitedly to Michael about each and every one.

"This big white rock—we're gonna use it for a doorstop, Mom says. And this is my favorite." He scrambled to his feet and went to the table where Michael was having breakfast. He held out a shell. "See? Isn't it beautiful? The pink and the gray and the purple—just like a rainbow."

Joanna was touched by her son's sensitivity, and his facility with words. Michael ought to appreciate that. But Michael seemed completely disinterested, even when one of Casey's small hands casually drifted onto his shoulder. Joanna's stomach knotted at her son's unthinking affection.

But then she saw the fine stream of sand drizzling down from the shell onto Michael's toast, and she clapped a hand to her mouth to stop a cry.

To her undying relief, Michael said nothing. His eyes just lifted icily to hers.

"I'm sorry," she mouthed quietly. "Come on, Casey. Help me hang the laundry." She took her son's hand, the hand that held the shell, and coaxed him away. "Meg, the lady we met yesterday, has invited you over to play with her children today."

Casey tried to pull his hand free, a slightly rebellious look in his eyes. In the process, the shell slipped from his fingers and hit the floor. Before he could check his step, his foot descended right on top of it. He jumped back, but too late. The shell was shattered. Suddenly his lower lip began to tremble.

Joanna stooped and quickly swept the pieces into her hand. "It was only a shell, Casey. We can find lots more like it."

Casey had always been the sort of child who took disappointment in stride. But since Phil's death, he'd sometimes had difficulty accepting other, smaller losses. Today he would not be consoled. He raised a hand over his face and began to cry, quietly, sadly, barely making any noise. Only his shoulders shook.

Joanna clapped the shell dust into the wastebasket, then scooped her son up into her arms. "Shh! Shh!" she soothed, carrying him out to the front porch. "We have a whole summer to collect shells, love. We'll find lots more, hundreds of them. We'll have to rent a trailer just to carry back our shells."

She decided to forget about the laundry. She could always hang it later. "Why don't we take a ride over to Meg's right now and meet her little boy Paul? I hear he collects Matchbox cars just like you do." It took a full five minutes before she succeeded in getting Casey's mind off the shell. But finally she was able to set him back down on his feet.

"Okay, you go wait in the car. I'll be right back. I just have to get my bag and shopping list from the kitchen."

Joanna ran back inside. Michael had left, undoubtedly disgusted by Casey's behavior. He'd also left the shells littering the floor.

CASEY AND MEG'S SON had little trouble getting acquainted. Joanna left them engrossed in a game of Chutes and Ladders, then drove to the market to buy her share of the week's groceries.

Two hours later she was back at the cottage. Michael's car, a surprisingly sensible Volvo, was gone. She put away the groceries, picked up the shells and hung the laundry. With that done, she went upstairs to make the beds.

The door to Michael's room was open. His bed had been made but with masculine haste and ineptness. For a moment she felt the urge to go in and straighten it out. In fact, her foot was already in the room before the shock of what she was doing hit her. What had ever possessed her? Michael didn't deserve the slightest gesture of help or kindness from her.

Joanna leaned in the doorway and let her gaze wander around the room. Inadvertently her memory wandered, too—back to the night her father and Viv had told her about Bunny's pregnancy. Some time during that awful night, she had crept across the dark hall from her room to this one, and in her desolation had crawled into that bed. What a pathetic little thing Michael had reduced her to, hugging the sheets to her sob-racked breast as if she might extract a bit of him from the cold material. She had stayed there until the sky lightened—and she began to realize he was not coming home. Then she'd risen and carefully remade the bed, erasing any traces that she'd been there.

Michael hadn't even had the decency to come home and face her that night. He hadn't called to offer even a minimal apology. So why had she just felt that appalling urge to go in and straighten his bed?

Joanna felt a throbbing behind her eyes and knew her face was probably pinched with worry. Were there feelings she didn't know about, didn't even suspect, lying beneath the surface of her life along with all the unresolved anger and pain? At the moment, however, the last thing Joanna wanted to do was start asking herself uncomfortable questions. She closed the door to Michael's room and ran down the stairs as if pursued.

THOUGH SHE HAD THE HOUSE all to herself and could have sat and read a book or gone out to lie in the sun, Joanna was still too edgy to relax. To get her mind off Michael and their untenable living arrangement, she hauled out the vacuum cleaner and dust cloth and gave the house a thorough cleaning.

Meg brought Casey back around three, and Michael returned shortly after that. Evidently he'd been shopping, too, for typewriter ribbons and paper. He set his bag down on the gleaming dining-room table and gave the place a slow appraisal. He was scowling when Joanna came down the stairs, lugging the vacuum.

"You've been cleaning," his rich baritone rumbled.

"How perceptive!"

"The whole house?"

"All but your room." The day was hot and muggy, and Joanna's topknot had fallen out. The ponytail that resulted was now sticking to her neck. Her navy shorts and white tank top clung uncomfortably.

"What happened to doing our own chores?" he asked derisively.

"I couldn't figure out how to divide the downstairs rooms. We all use them. So I decided we can alternate their cleaning."

Michael chuckled scornfully. "Nice to know you still like to make all the rules."

"And what's that supposed to mean?"

"Not a damn thing, Joanna." The heat was getting to him, too. A few dark curls clung to his forehead and he exuded a musky male scent that was not unattractive. He picked up his purchases and headed for the stairs. Halfway up, he turned and leaned over the banister. "Are you still planning to go out tonight?"

"Yes."

"Did you find someone to stay with Casey?"

"Yesss! Don't worry about it."

"Oh, I'm not worried. I just wanted to remind you that I won't be available."

"I know that!"

"Okay, okay. I don't want to get into another target shoot." He raised a hand as if warding her off—now that he'd succeeded in riling her thoroughly. "Just so long as you know." With that, he continued up the stairs and disappeared into his room.

"Ma?" Casey called timidly. She turned, startled. He must have been on the sun porch during the whole exchange.

"Ma, how come you and Uncle Michael fight so much?"

The question caught her off guard. Casey was obviously more aware of the tension in the house than she'd thought.

"Don't worry about what Michael and I say to each other, love. We're just...just teasing most of the time." She bit her lip, hoping he would accept the excuse.

Children were so perceptive. She had thought she and Michael were masking the tension between them well, at least in front of Casey. But she was beginning to fear that it had been evident all along—and worse, that it was growing, day by day, like a head of steam.

NATHAN CAME BY promptly at seven. They picked up Meg and Steve and then went on to Edgartown. Joanna was nervous at first but soon realized her apprehension was totally unfounded. Nathan was an easy person to get along with, and his humor was dwarfed only by his sister's. They ate at an elegant little restaurant, then went on to the Hot Tin Roof, the popular night spot owned by singer Carly Simon who, like many other celebrities, had a home on the Vineyard.

Joanna had a lovely evening. For the first time in months, she even felt attractive. She had worn her white sundress with the red piping and white T-strapped heels. She'd swept her hair up into a loose twist and applied makeup with a careful, delicate hand since her complexion was already glowing from the sun.

All in all, though, she was glad it was a weeknight and the men had to get up early for work the next day. They were back at the cottage by eleven o'clock.

"Would you like to come in for coffee?" she asked politely. Nathan was opening her door. He had brought her home first, and she suspected it was a deliberate move to ease any fear she might have that he would pressure her for a good-night kiss. His sensitivity was touching.

"I'd love a cup," Meg sang, feeling the effects of too many rum-and-cokes.

"Honey, do you know what time it is?" Steve asked. He was a mild-natured man, as quiet as Meg was outspoken.

"Yes, I do. It's early and I'd love a cup of coffee."

"So would I," Nathan added.

"Good," Joanna laughed. "Come on in."

Meg literally danced up the stairs, singing the song the band had been playing when they'd left the bar. On the porch, she threw her arms around Nathan and Joanna. "Have I told you yet how cute you two look together?"

Nathan shot Joanna a quick, amused look. "A few times."

"I mean it. Don't you think they make an adorable couple, Steve?" She slurred her words slightly as they entered the kitchen. Her husband groaned.

"Don't be embarrassed," Joanna said. "That's what I like about Meg. You always know what's on her mind." Suddenly her smile froze. Michael was sitting at the small Formica table, deep in a game of cribbage with the babysitter. There was no way he couldn't have heard their entrance.

"Michael!" Meg exclaimed, rushing over and giving him a hug. "It's so good to see you again." From the corner of her eye, Joanna could see Nathan tense.

Michael put his cards down slowly. "Good to see you, too, Meg." His eyes swept over the others, stopping to linger on Joanna. He hadn't seen her before she'd left. He'd stayed in his room, door firmly shut, all the time she was getting ready. Now those eyes swept over her with a thoroughness that caused a rushing in her ears.

"How w-was Casey tonight?" she asked quickly.

The baby-sitter rose reluctantly. There was a flush to her complexion that gave Joanna the distinct impression she already had a crush on Michael.

"Oh, just fine. We played for a while, then we put him to bed. No trouble."

We? Joanna searched Michael's face, but it remained impassive. She opened her bag and dug out her wallet to pay the girl.

"Can I give you a lift home?"

"Oh, no thanks. I brought my moped," she replied. But if Michael had asked, Joanna thought with amusement, she would've forgotten she even owned such a thing.

Once the baby-sitter was gone, Joanna put on a pot of coffee and invited them all into the living room. Much to her relief, Michael rose and excused himself from their company. A moment later she heard the back screen door clatter.

They moved into the living room and Joanna had barely settled herself into the club chair next to Nathan's when Meg said, "You know, seeing you and Michael together there in the kitchen really brought back memories."

Suddenly the walls seemed to close in on her.

"Memories? What memories?" Steve asked.

"Oh, Michael and Joanna mostly. They were quite a pair the last time I saw them."

Steve looked perplexed. "Did you two date? I thought you were related."

Dread gripped her heart. She and Michael were a subject Joanna definitely did not want to delve into with these people.

"Did they date?" Meg exclaimed. "Why, those two were so much in love—sorry, Nate—that I could feel the heat from this house clear across the pond." She turned to Joanna laughingly. "There were more girls around here who wanted to tear your eyes out! But then . . ." A puzzled look filtered into her slightly unfocused eyes. "All of a sudden you were gone without even saying goodbye to anyone, and the next thing I knew, Michael was marrying that awful Bunny Wilcox and you were marrying a guy up north. Boy, if that didn't have the island buzzing!"

Leave it to Meg, Joanna thought with a silent groan. In her guileless way, Meg had brought up the very issue she'd been trying to avoid for the past three days—maybe even

for the past six years, if she were perfectly honest. But, of
course, she'd been thinking about little else, arguing with
herself in the dark recesses of the night, trying out expressions, rearranging answers. What attitude should she take
if the subject came up? What reasons could she give if she
bumped into an old friend?

She took a deep breath and tried to relax. After all, it
wasn't as if this were the first time. There had been her father and Viv...and Phil's parents...and her mother, of
course. But that all seemed so long ago...

"What a memory you have, Meg!" she said, laughing as
casually as she could. "I'd nearly forgotten about all that."
She rolled her eyes as if suffering mild embarrassment over
some minor girlhood experience.

Nathan fidgeted uncomfortably in the other easy chair,
glowering at his sister, who didn't notice it.

"We were just kids, Michael and I," Joanna continued.
"I was just one of his many dates, and he was just one of
mine. All in all, considering the entire scope of our lives, it
was a rather insignificant few months."

"Didn't seem all that insignificant at the time." Meg
laughed uneasily.

"Good grief, if a girl married every guy she thought she
was in love with, the world would be in a state of bedlam."

"As if it isn't already." Meg's eyes still looked troubled.
"I suppose you know best what you felt but—it was just
strange. There was a rumor that Bunny..." She shook her
head and let the thought trail off.

"That Bunny was pregnant?" Joanna said quietly,
fighting the tightening in her chest. Meg nodded. "And if
Bunny was pregnant, then I must have married Phil on the
rebound? Yes, I imagined there would be rumors like that."

"Meg, why don't we forget the coffee?" Nathan said,
smiling sympathetically at Joanna. "I'm sure Joanna
doesn't want to dredge up—"

"No, really, it's all right," Joanna said almost adamantly. "It was nothing like that. Nothing at all. Actually
my marriage to Phil was as inevitable as night following

day. I don't suppose any of the rumors included the fact that I'd been dating him for four years."

Meg looked up. "Four years! Really, Jo?"

"Really," she emphasized, feeling the ache in her chest tighten even more. But her pride was at stake; she couldn't let down her guard now. Besides, there was Casey—and Phil's memory—and she loved them simply too much to let them appear a cheap consolation prize she'd turned to at a low swing in her life. "Michael was just a...a summertime kind of thing. A lot of heat, but over in a few months—if you know what I mean." She tried to laugh lightly. "Phil was the constant in my life all along. When I went home after that summer here, I realized how much I'd missed him, and we decided to get married right away. Maybe Michael was good for me—you know, someone to test my love for Phil. But that's all he was. My marriage was definitely not something I rushed into on the rebound."

"I see," Meg said. "I should have known."

"That's all right. How could you?" Joanna sensed her audience was convinced. She sat back, exhausted, realizing only now how tense she had been.

But somehow she had survived the ordeal. She'd reconstructed the past and made her company see only what she wanted them to see. She was amazed, if not a little horrified, at how thoroughly she had done it, too. There had been moments when she'd almost lost track of the truth herself.

She rubbed her eyes tiredly. At times, she sounded so like her mother—that same cold pride and uncompromising independence that stemmed from being hurt by a man. It was frightening.

"What did you say?" Joanna lifted her head, suddenly realizing that Nathan had been speaking.

"...about you two sharing the cottage this summer. Let's face it, if what people said was true, you and Michael certainly wouldn't be able to live here now without bitterness, right?"

Joanna caught the drift of his words and felt her face flushing. "Oh, right. Of course. That coffee smells about ready," she interjected quickly, rising from the chair.

"Let me help." Nathan was immediately on his feet, too.

Conversation seemed a blur of inanities to Joanna until her company left, which, blessedly, was soon after the coffee was drunk. When they were gone, she put the cups in the sink. Then she tiptoed back through the living and dining rooms, turning off lights as she headed for the stairs. She longed for the refuge of her bed. The conversation tonight had taken more out of her than she'd realized. Maybe tomorrow she would be able to ignore what Meg had forced her to remember. Maybe tomorrow she would be able to go on pretending that the lies she'd told them were the truth. But not tonight. She was as aware of her love for Michael and the devastation it had brought her as if the years that had intervened were just a matter of days.

In a way, she thought, it was a shame she and Michael had never had the opportunity to confront each other. Maybe if she'd been able to vent her anger, spill out her feelings, get him to admit he was wrong—maybe all of this would be out of her system by now. But they hadn't. Nothing had ever been resolved. It had just been buried under the happiness and the busyness and, yes, especially the sadness of what followed.

But she couldn't tamp down those feelings any longer. Not tonight anyway. Here she was on Martha's Vineyard again, sharing the cottage with a very real Michael Malone, and as if that weren't enough to bring the past to life, tonight she'd had to endure Meg's recollections.

She was sure she'd be all right in the morning. All she needed was time to mend. Somewhere in the night, she would find the uncaring, independent attitude she had donned after leaving here six years ago. All she needed was rest, and then no one, not even Michael, would be able to make her feel this vulnerable again.

CHAPTER SIX

JUST AS SHE REACHED the stairs, Michael's tall frame detached itself from the darkness of the sun porch. Her heart leaped to her throat. She had been under the impression that he'd gone out.

"Sorry, I didn't mean to startle you."

"You didn't," she lied. He looked dark and ominous and unfairly huge. She wished she could get her feet to move but they suddenly seemed paralyzed.

"Did you enjoy yourself tonight?"

"W-what?"

"On your date."

"Oh, that! Yes." Her fingers played fretfully with the folds of her skirt. "We went to...to the Hot Tin Roof."

"Well, he seems a nice enough guy." Michael's hair was rumpled over his forehead. The dim lamplight cast shadows into the hollows of his cheeks. "He used to have a crush on you, didn't he?" His voice was liquid with a predatory sweetness she didn't trust.

"I guess." She shrugged.

"You guess? And are you aware that he still does?"

Silence shifted uneasily between them.

"I don't think it's fair to jump to that conclusion," she said defensively.

"It wasn't much of a jump. His eyes kept following you like a mindless little puppy's."

Joanna stared at Michael, unable to control the turbulent feelings rising inside her. "I don't appreciate your talking about Nathan like that. He and I had a wonderful time tonight. It did me a world of good to get out, and if he

decides he'd like to go out again, I'd feel honored." In her
agitation, she had taken a step closer to Michael, close
enough to smell the clean, warm fragrance of his body.

He raised his hands in mock surrender. "Okay, Jo. I'm
sorry. It doesn't matter to me what you do or who you go
out with. You go your way, I go mine, etcetera, etcetera."

"Good!"

"Fine!"

Joanna's chest rose and fell like a bellows. If she knew
what was good for her, she would get up to her room right
now. She didn't want to start anything with Michael now,
not strung out the way she was from that dreadful conversation. She felt out of control, stripped of her defenses. She
wasn't sure what she would say or where her feelings might
take her.

She had turned and climbed two stairs when Michael's
smooth, sardonic voice cut through her resolve.

"If you want to go out dancing and carousing so soon
after your husband's death, that's entirely up to you."

Joanna's feet froze to the stair tread. She closed her eyes
and groaned. For some unfathomable reason, Michael
seemed determined to keep them on a collision course.

Well, maybe he was right. Maybe they'd been playing
their silly game too long. Maybe it was time she gave him
an honest piece of her mind!

She stomped down the stairs and pushed him out to the
sun porch where their voices wouldn't carry up to Casey.
"For your information, Michael Malone, my husband died
nearly eight months ago! What am I supposed to do, dress
in sackcloth and ashes all my life?"

"Of course not. But isn't it traditional to wait at least a
year? Or doesn't that stuff matter to you? Maybe this
wasn't even the first time you went out."

Joanna's fists tightened at her sides. "I have no idea what
your problem is, but my affairs are none of your business."

He lifted his head and laughed contemptuously. Starlight, coming through the windows, streaked the bridge of

his arrogant nose and deepened the furrows of his brow. "Isn't that a revealing choice of words!"

Joanna stared at him dumbfoundedly for a moment before she felt the color drain from her face. Then she grabbed up a pillow from a chair and flung it at him with all her strength.

But Michael's reflexes were quick and he deflected the missile easily. "Stop it, Joanna!" he ordered, taking a threatening step forward.

"Apologize for that insinuation first!"

"Why should I? Evidently affairs are your specialty. You admitted it to your friends in the living room just a few minutes ago."

"What?" she shrieked incredulously. Had he been in the sun porch the whole time? Suddenly the conversation with her guests took on nightmarish proportions.

"Oh, I'll admit, you had me fooled that summer, but then I didn't know what a good little actress you were." Though his voice remained level, his fingers tightened on the back of a chair until they turned white.

"What are you talking about?" Joanna whispered frantically, wishing she could transport herself to the safety of her room.

"Don't play the little innocent with me, Jo! I've seen that performance before and frankly, it's getting a little stale. I'm talking about the summer before you got married. You *do* remember that summer, don't you? The summer you and your friends just had such a laugh over? Or did it mean so little that it's slipped your mind already?"

The shadows of the room swam before Joanna's eyes until she thought she would faint. "I...I remember," she whispered weakly. "But I seem to recall it as the summer before *you* got married, Michael."

Michael's eyes swept over her disdainfully. "May I ask what the hell you thought you were doing that summer?"

She averted her eyes, remembering what she'd said to Meg and the others.

"What did you think you were doing?" he repeated. With each word, his voice rose until it was a nerve-shattering explosion. Joanna clapped her hands over her ears, but he tore them away, glaring at her with a coldness she had never dreamed him capable of.

"What were you trying to prove, pretending you were in love with me," he continued, "when all the while you were planning to marry someone else?" He pointed out the window as if that someone else were just beyond the nearest bush.

Joanna's eyes opened wide with shock. Not only had she convinced the others about the shallowness of her feelings that summer, but she had convinced Michael, too. Incredible as it seemed, he believed every last word. And he was furious!

It didn't make any sense. Somehow, everything had become twisted around over the years. She hadn't the foggiest idea why it should matter to him now—unless his ego was so big he couldn't stand the idea of learning, however late, that he'd once been made the fool? But it didn't matter. Late or not, Michael was genuinely upset.

For a moment she felt the wildest urge to tell him the truth and set things right. But she would be a fool to do that. Why shouldn't he feel some of the pain of rejection *she* had felt six years ago? Let him think she'd walked away from here unscathed. Whatever he felt, it would be nothing compared to what she had suffered.

"What were you doing all those times we made love?" he continued to demand, leaning so close she could feel the angry trembling of his body.

She stared into his cobalt eyes and was suddenly overwhelmed by the memories she saw reflected in them. Just as suddenly, she was gripped by an incomprehensible sadness, a grief for those profoundly happy days that had been snuffed out by his treachery. She tore her eyes from his and turned away, weak and trembling.

"I'm serious. I'd like to know." He gripped her arm and swung her around again. "Were you unsure of yourself as a woman? Were you trying to learn about lovemaking with me so you wouldn't disappoint the guy you were really planning to marry?'' With his free hand, he again pointed out the window. ''Or were you just looking for a summer of kicks before you settled down?''

The conversation was turning into a nightmare of distortions. Where did he get such notions? And why was he probing so cruelly? Why couldn't he just let the past rest in peace?

''Michael, I don't want to talk about this anymore.'' She made a move toward the door, but his hand tightened on her arm.

''What's the matter? The truth too hard to face?''

Joanna winced. Suddenly something inside her seemed to shudder—and snap. ''The truth? The truth? Michael, you wouldn't know the truth if it hit you between the eyes.'' This time when she tried to yank free of his grip, she succeeded. But instead of backing away and heading for the door as she'd intended, she took a bold step closer, her face tilted defiantly toward his. She was trembling from head to foot with newfound anger.

''The truth is you've never been capable of loving anybody but yourself, Michael. You've always been that way— irresponsible, self-serving, drunk on your own appeal. I knew it the first time I met you, and I was only sixteen at the time. You never gave a damn about me. I just attracted you because I was an innocent kid. And the only reason you're angry now is that your pride is hurt. You're asking yourself, 'Gee, why couldn't I break this girl's heart the way I broke so many others? Why didn't she fall to pieces when I threw her over for somebody else?' ''

Michael's eyes narrowed. He went very still. ''Is that what you think of me?''

''That's what I *know* about you, buster!'' she returned, her strength continuing to rise. ''Oh, I'll admit, I let down my guard for a while that summer. But then, I was a little out of my league tangling with you. In fact, I didn't have a chance. There I was, an inexperienced country kid, and you . . . you were a past master at seduction." Her words seemed to have a mind of their own, as if they were all spilling out after years of being repressed.

"Seduction?"

"That's right. With your slick lines about feeling married to me, and all those grand promises about our future together." For a moment, her strength failed her and she felt herself swaying. "No, Michael, I wasn't experimenting with sex and I wasn't just out for kicks," she said sadly, feeling that inexplicable sense of loss again. "You seduced me into making love. It's as simple and tragic as that."

Michael's eyes widened and he gasped a halfhearted, bitter laugh. "Is that so? Well, if it was seduction, you certainly didn't give me much of an argument."

Rational thought abandoned her, and all the feelings she had denied since leaving here came roiling to the surface.

"Are you trying to say I—I was *easy*? When you were out behind my back sleeping with Bunny Wilcox—sleeping with half the girls on the island, for all I know!" She could feel her nails digging painfully into her palms. "You have a nerve to stand there and criticize *me* the first time I see another man after being faithful to my husband and his memory for five and a half years!" Emotion was mounting so rapidly, she was actually seeing red spots in front of her.

Michael continued to glare down at her, his expression so cold and derisive she wondered if he was really the same person she had once loved and found so charming and compassionate.

"Faithful? You don't know the meaning of the word, Joanna! Tell me, how soon will it be before you let ol' Nathan give you a tumble?"

Without realizing what she was doing, Joanna raised her hand and sent it cracking across his face. The derisive smile dropped from his lips and his eyes went black and fiery. A split second later, she felt a hard palm come smacking across her own cheek.

Tears sprang to her eyes and a voice within warned her that she should be frightened. But she wasn't. She was merely seeing his appalling treatment of her with deeper clarity, feeling the pain of his deceit with renewed sharpness—and falling further and further into the depths of her pent-up fury.

"Don't you dare hit me!" she fired back, green eyes flashing. She pushed his chest hard, wanting to knock him down and pummel him with her bare fists. She could almost taste the satisfaction it would bring.

But her efforts were meaningless. Michael caught her wrists and pinned them behind her back.

"Let me go," she rasped. She struggled against him and temporarily lost her balance, tottering on her high-heeled shoes.

"Not until I'm damn well ready to, my love," he taunted, crushing her against him.

Joanna couldn't stand feeling so helpless, being imprisoned in his arms, feeling the heat and powerful strength of his body trembling through hers. She could hardly think coherently anymore. She was simply a mass of nerve ends and pumping adrenaline.

With all the desperation of a cornered animal, she raised her foot and jammed it down along the inside of his shins.

He winced and his body felt heavy against hers, as if it were momentarily boneless. Again she felt herself tipping out of balance. This time, however, Michael was unable to set her right. This time her knees buckled and she fell backward, Michael's heavy weight going with her.

She hit the floor with a bone-crushing thud. She gasped, first to catch the breath that had been knocked out of her, and then in reaction to the pain that nearly paralyzed her body. Fresh tears filled her eyes.

Michael had fallen, too, Joanna cushioning much of his fall. As if his weight weren't bad enough, one of his arms was still wrapped around her, digging agonizingly into her back. She tried to move to free his arm but every ounce of strength seemed to have left her.

"Get off me. I can't breathe." The words were difficult, made breathless by her suppressed sobs.

Michael slid his arms out from under her and slowly lifted himself up onto one elbow. Still stunned, he shook his head, then rubbed his forehead. Joanna began to wonder if he had knocked it on the floor when he hit.

"Are you all right?" she whispered.

He nodded. "You?"

"I don't know. Yes ... I guess."

Michael's eyes swept over her. She could feel tears trickling down the sides of her face. With a low moan, he lowered his head and buried his face in her long tangled hair.

"What have we done to each other, Joanna?" he whispered raggedly. "What have we done?" He lay very still, with an exhausted heaviness throughout his body.

Joanna lay beneath him, sobbing quietly.

After a while, he dragged himself up and without looking at her, held out a hand. She noticed it was trembling. Slowly she lifted hers and let him help her up. Her dress was twisted and torn. Her hair hung like a tattered mop.

"Michael?" she whispered tremulously.

He looked up and starlight silvered his handsome, anguished face. It lit his dark, wavy hair, made sensuous the sad, drooping mouth. His long eyelashes were wet.

Joanna felt a thousand emotions in that moment—most of them illogical. But the one that disturbed her most was the compassion she suddenly felt. This was no casual case of a womanizer's wounded pride. Michael had been hurt. He had genuinely suffered. Though she still didn't understand it, he was wrestling with a pain, an anger, that very much resembled her own. At that moment she felt so unutterably bad for him her heart ached.

"Uh ... nothing." She drew back, alarmed. This was no time to start feeling sorry for Michael Malone! She had come too far. She couldn't allow herself to lose ground now. It was...too late!

She turned on wobbly legs and went up to her room. There, she pulled her suitcase from under her bed and in the dark began to empty her dresser.

CHAPTER SEVEN

"JUST GET IN THE CAR and stop asking questions," Joanna snapped uncharacteristically the next morning. Her son glared from under the veil of his dark lashes and obeyed. Joanna bit her lip guiltily. She had been bullying him all morning—rushing him through breakfast, barking at him when he'd tried to sneak up to Michael's room.

"But where are we going?" he asked, trying to tie his sneaker as the car lurched down the driveway.

She didn't answer—couldn't answer—knowing the disappointment her reply would bring.

Fifteen minutes later, she was standing inside the Steamship Authority, reading the ferry schedule on the wall. Good. There was a boat leaving at one, which would give her plenty of time to pack the rest of her things.

"Ma, why are we here?" Casey persisted, tugging at her hand.

Joanna glanced down at his wary face. She knelt down and took him by the waist. "Casey, I'm ready to go home now. I . . ."

Before she could say anything else, his lower lip began to tremble. "But I don't want to go yet."

"Casey, please don't argue. We can't stay here forever."

"I know, but we just got here."

Joanna sighed impatiently. "Stop it! We're going and that's all there is to it."

"No!" he wailed. A few people nearby turned and gave Joanna censorious looks. "I didn't buy Grandma a present yet. And we never went out to the other island."

"Nantucket?" she said, remembering a promise she had made before they'd come. "Some other time, babe." She tried to soothe him, but he wriggled away.

"Leave me alone!" he hollered.

Joanna's face flushed. Casey had never pulled a tantrum before, at home or in public. What was the matter with him? What was he doing to her?

She paused abruptly. What was he doing to *her*? The question was, what was she doing to *him*? Had she taken leave of her senses? Did she really want to take him away from all this—the lazy timelessness of the sea, the joy he found playing in the sand, wandering through meadows of wildflowers, meeting new playmates who bore no association with the grief he had suffered?

Then why was she running away? And running it was, she realized. Did Michael still hold so much power over her that he could send her fleeing for the nearest ship even now? Well, Michael Malone could go straight to hell! Even if he tormented her to skin and bones, she would not leave. Casey meant far too much to her.

"Yes, may I help you?" the ticket agent asked.

"Oh, no thanks."

He looked at her quizzically.

"Come on, Casey," she said, scooping him up. "Sometimes I think you have more sense than I do."

"Are we going home?"

"No, we're heading back to the cottage."

Casey flung his arms around her neck and pressed his wet cheek to hers. "That's what I meant, Ma!" He giggled with trembling relief.

There was a large manila envelope on the kitchen table when she returned. It was addressed to her, with her mother's return address in the corner. Evidently Michael was up and stirring and had gone out for the mail.

She poured herself a glass of lemonade, then opened the envelope. Inside was a short note from her mother and a copy of the weekly hometown paper, which Joanna had asked Dorothy to forward. She sat down and opened the paper to the job ads.

"Good morning," a husky voice called from the door.

"Nathan! Hi, come on in."

"What are you doing?" He collapsed into the chair opposite her.

"Just browsing through the want ads."

He reached across the table and lifted the drooping front page so he could read the masthead. "You interested in a new job?"

She shrugged. "I'm thinking about it."

"Good Lord, why? Hasn't your life been crazy enough this past year?"

"Can I get you something to drink?"

"No, thanks. So why are you looking for another job?"

She sighed wearily. "To put it in a nutshell, money. Don't get me wrong, we're getting by, but just barely. I'd like to do so much more for Casey."

Nathan scratched his thick beard and stared at her thoughtfully. "Come work for me then."

Joanna nearly choked on her lemonade. "What?"

"That's right. I'm looking for someone to fill a managerial position at my Edgartown shop, and I think you'd be perfect. You have experience, you're career minded, and you like retail work, don't you?"

"Yes," she admitted hesitantly. "But that would mean I'd have to live here permanently."

A smile lit Nathan's rugged face. "That's the basic idea."

She laughed. "I'll have to think about it."

"All kidding aside, I'm really strapped for help. And I'd pay a good salary, with medical coverage, a pension plan, and lots of other fringe benefits." He leered comically.

"Thanks. I mean that," she said, hoping her voice conveyed her appreciation. "But I was thinking of something—well, more professional, something I might have to go back to school for."

"You're thinking about returning to school?"

"Possibly." And before he could remind her again how turbulent her life had been, "What brings you here today? I thought you'd be working."

"I fully intended to, but it's too nice a day. How would you like to go out for a boat ride?"

"You have a boat?"

"A small cabin cruiser. I keep it docked at Menemsha."

Joanna smiled, having discovered something to keep her out of the house for the day. "Sure, why not?"

"Great. Go grab your gear and your son, and we'll be off."

"Casey?" Joanna called as she hurried up the stairs. He had told her he would be up in their room playing with his Lego blocks, but when she looked in, he wasn't there. From across the hall, his high, thin giggle sent a shiver down her back. *Michael's room.*

She pushed open the door and there he was, perched on Michael's lap at the desk. Neither of them heard her enter.

"Good. What comes next?" Michael's head was bent close to the boy's.

"*H*. I know, it's *H*," Casey said, his voice brimming with boastful delight. "But I can't find it. Oh. Oh, here it is!" His finger hovered over the typewriter, then clumsily smashed down a key. He leaned his head back against Michael's shoulder and laughed with the pride of accomplishment.

"Now *I*," Michael prompted.

"I *know. I J K L M N O P*," he recited in a rush.

Joanna wondered how long Casey had been with Michael. She hoped he hadn't said anything about their trip to the ferry landing.

"Casey, what are you doing in here?"

He turned in surprise. "I'm typing, Ma. Just like Uncle Michael."

Joanna hadn't seen Michael all morning, and even now he didn't turn toward her. She wondered if he felt as embarrassed about last night's battle as she did.

"I've told you a dozen times not to disturb Michael while he's working." For a moment she wished she had her son's vantage point and could see what that "work" actually was.

"I know. What do you want, Ma?" Casey wound an arm around Michael's neck and rested his chin on the man's shoulder.

"I want you to come over here right now and stop bothering him."

"I'm sorry." But he still didn't move.

"Nathan's going to take us for a boat ride today."

"A boat ride?" He considered the proposal, then slid off Michael's lap and walked to his mother.

"Sorry he disturbed you," she said curtly to the back of Michael's head.

"No bother."

Joanna's eyes snapped wide open. It sounded as if he almost meant it.

It was a wonderful afternoon, and the boat was a dream, a sumptuous forty-foot cabin cruiser with all the amenities of a home. It was just what Joanna needed to forget the clash of the previous night.

But it was impossible to forget completely. Now that she was determined to stay, she would have to face the dilemma of living with Michael all over again, and this time on a new plateau of difficulty. Last evening the polite facade they'd been hiding behind since she'd arrived had finally been stripped away. Now their feelings were out in the open, all the raw wounds and accusations. Where had she stored all that anger and hatred during her happy marriage? How had she ignored the pain for so long and convinced herself she felt nothing for Michael?

It still startled her to think that Michael was hurt and angry, too. After all, *he* had two-timed *her*; there was nothing for him to be angry about—except that he really believed *she* had two-timed *him* while Phil waited in the wings, or some such nonsense. But even more puzzling was the fact that it saddened her so much. This strange pity stealing over her, this compassion for his anguish—where was it coming from? And why? He didn't deserve it.

She spent the afternoon lounging in a deck chair—and trying not to think about Michael—while Nathan piloted the boat through the Elizabeth Islands and around Buzzard's Bay. They docked at the old whaling city of New Bedford and had lunch at a restaurant overlooking the modern fishing fleet. Later, they strolled the narrow, cobbled streets of the newly restored historic district, stopped into an antique shop, and even found time to tour the whaling museum.

"Can I take you two out to dinner?" Nathan asked as they docked back at Menemsha. The sun was already riding low on the horizon.

"Thanks. It's been a wonderful day, but I'd like to get home."

"Mmm. I understand. Bouncing around in a boat can be awfully tiring."

Joanna smiled, glad for the ready excuse. Actually she wasn't tired at all. In fact, her whole body was running on overdrive now that she was heading home and back to Michael. All day she'd been worried about returning to the house and risking a repeat of last night's argument.

Suddenly she thought of a solution. It wasn't a permanent one, but at least it would get her through one more night and buy her a little time.

JOANNA AND CASEY pitched the old canvas tent in the sheltered hollow of a dune. Then they walked the dusky beach, gathering driftwood. As night sifted down from the gold and pink clouds, they sat by a cozy fire roasting hot dogs on the ends of long sticks. The thicket of beach plum rustled with a slight wind. The tall grass whistled. And over it all, the sea murmured its incessant low roar.

They didn't say much. Casey just sat watching the flames, and Joanna sat watching Casey. How she adored this child! No one could ever come close to guessing.

And yet there were times when she knew he couldn't fill all her emotional needs. Like now. There was an empty spot inside that she didn't fully understand, a need to share her thoughts and problems, her anxieties and joys.

Oh, why did Phil have to die? Why did her safe little world have to fall apart? It had been such a comfort and a refuge.

But what had it been a refuge from?

The evening was growing cool and damp. She zippered Casey's sweatshirt and tugged up the hood.

"Aw, Ma!" he laughed, shrugging away. Something pulled at her heart strings. He was growing too quickly, maturing from her baby into a boy. Day by day, she could see changes in him, in his increasingly complex speech patterns, in the growing agility of his body.

But lately there were changes that disquieted her, too... like his stern refusal to cuff his jeans because Michael's had no cuffs... like the way he slouched in chairs, his feet barely reaching the windowsill, again because of Michael. And he had been under Michael's influence how long? Four days?

It wasn't that she begrudged Casey's admiration of another adult. There were lots of adults he loved and admired—his grandparents, aunts, uncles. It was just his admiring *this* adult that bothered her. Michael paid almost no attention to Casey. It was obvious he considered him a disturbance in the house. And the way he called him "kid," as if he had no name—as if Michael were trying to deny his very existence!

Then, what was this instinctive attraction Casey felt for Michael?

"Ma, your hot dog's burning," Casey cried.

Joanna shook herself out of her reverie. "Oh, it's all right, Case. They taste better this way. Will you get the buns, please?"

The child stood up and went to the picnic basket. The breeze, coming over the lip of the dune, caught his hair and whipped it back.

"Hurry, come sit," she said, feeling suddenly possessive and protective.

No, she didn't begrudge the wind, either—just what was blowing in the wind. No matter how hard she tried to avoid it, Michael was breezing his way back into her life. And Casey's.

Casey was exhausted and fell asleep before nine, but Joanna lay awake, staring up at the dark peak of canvas long after that. Her eyes were wide and restless. Finally she lifted herself out of her sleeping bag and unzipped the door. Outside, the night was still faintly luminescent, the air alive with rushing shore sounds. She wrapped her arms around her knees and listened.

She heard the crackle and spit of the dying fire, the soughing of the wind blowing sand over sand. And beyond the ridge of the dune, down the flat, damp beach, the waves rushed forward and back, forward and back.

She knew the beach was deserted, yet she had a feeling of something breathing out there, something immense and wonderful and eternal. It was a feeling she used to get when she was a girl, staring up at the stars or gazing across the mountains. But she'd always felt it most here, on this island of such varied and dramatic beauty.

Especially at Gay Head. She must take Casey out to Gay Head someday soon. The terrain there was wild and recklessly beautiful. It was a place of windswept moors, hills and hollows, and of course, the famous clay cliffs that rose 150 feet from the sea in dramatic striations of pink and yellow and mauve.

She and Michael used to love to drive out there in the evenings. In fact, it was the first place they went when she arrived that third and final summer. Inadvertently her mind drifted back... They had slipped through a gap in the fencing that was supposed to keep people off the eroding cliffs. Then they'd picked their way along a narrow path and sat at the edge of a steep drop, listening to the murmurous rush and retreat of the sea far below. A beam from a lighthouse stroked over them with its steady pulse.

"We shouldn't be out here," Joanna whispered guiltily. "This area's restricted."

"Good. Then we won't be disturbed."

"Michael, is this supposed to be a date?" She still wasn't sure if he meant what he'd written in his letter.

She felt his hand on her back, running up under her long, silky hair to her neck, his fingers stroking the smooth downy skin at her nape.

"If you want it to be," he answered softly, seductively.

She stared into his dark, languid eyes and felt as if she were tumbling off the cliff. Yes, she believed it; this was going to be their summer.

"I'd like that," she whispered.

He smiled. His head lowered and his lips found hers. His kiss was gentle, tentative, making no demands. But much to her alarm, she began to feel things, like the fluttering of tiny bird wings in her stomach. And when he drew away, she felt a wave of dismay.

He rose abruptly, the wind raking back his hair, and silently stared out over the ocean. Had she done something wrong? Had she disappointed him? Dear Lord, was he already getting bored?

He dug his hands into his pockets. "Joanna, this isn't right. Our parents are going to have a fit."

"Frankly I don't care."

"It's not only that. You're . . . you're too young."

"I'm eighteen!" All the love inside her was crying out in her anguished expression. If only he'd turn around, surely he would see it.

"A very young eighteen." His eyes narrowed as if against a deep pain.

"I know you're used to girls with more experience . . ."

"Not as much as you seem to think." He hung his head. "Nevertheless, I still don't deserve you. But I can't help myself. I can't get you out of my mind. . . ."

He looked so distraught, Joanna had to laugh. "Michael?" This time he did turn. She lay back and raised her arms to him, imploring him to come to her. "I'm not a

china doll, you know." She smiled adoringly, her lon
blond hair fanned out on the ground. "I'm not going t
break."

Even now, Joanna could still remember the way M
chael had caught his breath, the look that had come ove
his face. He'd lowered himself to his knees and gathered he
into his arms. This time when he kissed her, there was n
holding back, and she responded with a passion that wa
unlearned. It was as if the floodgates of womanly emotio
had been locked up tight until that moment.

Joanna shook herself out of her reverie. She couldn'
imagine what had started her thinking about that now
Granted, there were some very lovely memories ... but sh
had to remember Michael as the cold, self-serving two
timer he was at the end of that summer, not the person sh
had adored at the beginning.

Suddenly there was a flicker of white outside the un
zipped door. She jumped. What on earth ...? A sea gu
perhaps, flapping too near the tent?

It came again, and now she recognized it for what it was.
A man's handkerchief tied to the end of a stick.

"Joanna?"

"Michael?" she cried. It was as if her thoughts had con
jured him up bodily.

He laid down the white flag and peered into the tent. "Is
Casey asleep?"

"Yes."

"Good, I'd like to talk."

"Go away!" The night was suddenly pulsing against her
ears like the beating of a huge heart. It was difficult to
breathe. She couldn't see his face; the fire was behind him,
but she knew he was exasperated. She heard his impatient
huff.

"Joanna Scott, get out here!"

His voice held so much authority she decided to obey
without argument. The air was cool against her burning
cheeks, the sand beneath her damp as she scrambled to-

ard the fire. She huddled there sulkily and drew her
veatshirt closer.

"How did you know where to find us?" she asked as he
laced another piece of driftwood on the fire.

"This is where you and I always came when we wanted
) be alone." The ease with which he referred to their past
ook her by surprise. In fact, it was the first time either of
1em had referred to their past at all, apart from the dis-
ortions of last night.

He clapped the sand from his hands and settled across
he fire from her. Light flickered over his face, a face so
andsome Joanna sometimes felt an ache in her heart when
he looked at it. It seemed unfair that one man should
ossess so much appeal.

He flipped up the collar of his windbreaker. "You must
e crazy camping out on a night like this. The weatherman
ays it might even rain."

"Thanks for the warning, but you shouldn't have trekked
ll the way out here just for that."

"I didn't trek all the way out here just for that, and you
:now it." Their eyes locked, and Joanna's breathing went
hallow. He was up to something but she didn't know what.

"Not another brawl, I hope. Listen, Michael, if you
hink I get a thrill out of being mauled and manhan-
iled—"

"Will you be quiet?"

"What?"

"Please."

Joanna's mouth dropped open but nothing came out, so
deep was her surprise at the gentleness in his voice.

"Jo, I'm really sorry about last night. I've wanted to
apologize all day, but either you've been out or I just
haven't had the courage. I—I hope I didn't hurt you."

With a start, Joanna realized he was nervous. She shook
her head. "No, I wasn't hurt."

"Good." He sat without speaking, and yet she sensed
there was something trying to reach out from behind his
eyes.

Joanna cleared her throat. "Apology accepted. I wish I could also say forget it, but..."

"No, I don't want to forget it. What happened last night was too important to forget. I don't know what got into me. By the time your friends left, I was so angry at you I just couldn't control myself any longer. But rest assured, it won't happen again." His voice was becoming a lot more familiar to Joanna. It rang with the sincerity that belonged to the Michael she'd known years ago, one short eternal summer.

"You see," he continued, "ever since you arrived, I've been so tied up in knots trying to stay cool, I could hardly think. I guess overhearing that conversation with Meg was the last straw. But today..." He laughed with amazement. "Today I feel so much better. Lighter. You know?" His eyes raked over her, imploring her to understand. "It's as if last night was a necessary exorcism of something I've been carrying around for years. And today I've been going around with the strangest urge to talk."

"We talk."

"No, we don't. We hit and run. I don't think we've really talked since you got here."

Joanna's golden lashes fluttered nervously. Michael was looking at her, and his eyes were not hooded and flinty with deceit. They were clear and honest and imploring, and a bottomless feeling opened up in her stomach.

"Sooo!" He drew up his shoulders and dug his hands into his windbreaker pockets. "How the hell have you been, Joanna?"

She was reminded of all the other times he had asked her that same question and she'd either lied or lashed out. But she knew she could do no such thing now. It wasn't fair that he could make her feel so exposed, so vulnerable, especially after last night's argument. But then nothing that he had ever done was fair. Her shoulders slumped with defeat.

"I've been miserable," she confessed. "Really miserable."

Michael's smile broadened until his eyes crinkled, and suddenly Joanna couldn't keep from smiling, too. Being honest with him wasn't all that hard after all. In fact, it felt like a kind of release. Perhaps she'd exorcised a few demons of her own.

"Me, too," he admitted.

"No kidding?"

"No kidding."

She hesitated. "Is it ... your divorce?"

"My divorce..." He sighed reflectively. Then, "Hell, no! Getting Bunny out of my life was a relief! Our marriage was a farce. Besides, that's ancient history. We split up five years ago."

Joanna fell off the elbow she was leaning on. "You mean you were married only one year?"

"Less. What's the matter? Are you really all that surprised?"

Joanna could only laugh incredulously.

"No, what's really got me crazy is what I'm doing now. I—I quit teaching."

"You quit?" Joanna was still having trouble digesting the fact that Michael had been free for five years.

"Uh huh."

"But what was all that about a leave of absence?"

"I took a slight liberty with the truth."

"Wasn't it working out for you?" Suddenly she was sorry she'd ever wished failure on him. It had been such a small, mean-spirited sentiment.

"It was going very well."

"And are you really *Dr.* Malone?"

"Yes."

"Head of the Literature Department?"

His lips twitched with a small sheepish smile "That too." Though Joanna knew it was absurd, she felt a bubble of pride swell inside her.

"Things were going great. The school's literary journal was becoming nationally recognized...."

"Under your direction?"

He nodded again. "And a student-exchange program I'd been working on was finally gelling. I would've been traveling to Russia next year..."

Joanna rested her chin on her knees and let her imagination paint a picture of him as a college professor. He'd probably worn denims and tweed, she thought, and he'd probably left every female student starry-eyed by the end of the first lecture. Dynamic, passionately in love with his subject, humorous in an intellectual, offbeat way—yes, she could see him, his moves, his facial expressions. Could see him so clearly, in fact, that she felt a sharp pang of something absurdly akin to jealousy.

"And you quit?" she asked.

He nodded stolidly. "In May, as soon as the semester ended. It was one of the toughest decisions I've ever made. I really enjoyed academic life. But—but I love writing more."

Joanna's back straightened. So that was what he'd been working on up in his room!

"I finally realized I couldn't write and teach at the same time. Each one's too time-consuming. So I took the plunge."

"Writing?"

"Hmm. I know it doesn't make much sense, giving up the career I had. That's why I said I was on a leave of absence. But look at it this way, I now have only two choices. I can either succeed or I can fail, and I don't take too kindly to failure."

Joanna laughed incredulously.

"It isn't funny, Jo," he said, playfully swatting her leg. "I haven't a clue where I'm supposed to go from here if I don't succeed. I have a limited amount of money. I gave up my apartment in order to cut expenses. I even sold my furniture. The only things I kept were my car and my clothes. That's why—" he lowered his head "—why I need the cottage so badly this summer. The money. And because I need an environment of peace and tranquility in order to write."

Suddenly the full scope of his situation became clear. 'Oh, Michael! I had no idea. You should have told me.''

"It's really not so bad. Actually..." He began to smile. ''Actually it's pretty incredible. I'm finally doing what I always dreamed of doing, which is more than most people can say.''

"If I ask you what you're working on, will you tell me?''

"It's...a novel. Is that answer enough?''

An unexpected warmth swept through her and she smiled softly. "I should have known. You always were such a wonderful writer.''

His eyes glittered in the firelight. "Wasn't I just!'' They both laughed quietly. "I never thought it could be so hard, though. This piece is going slowly. I'm even beginning to wonder if I'll finish it on time.''

"On time?''

"Mmm. I have a deadline. The beginning of August.''

Joanna's nerves began to leap with excitement. "Does that mean...do you have a commitment from a publisher?''

He nodded, his smile growing. "Only because I have the most incredible agent. Her name's Joyce Sterling. She's with the Miles Carson Agency. You've probably heard of them. Really high-powered...?''

Joanna cocked her head warily. "Is that the same Joyce you talked to on the phone about a plumber?''

"Oh, you overheard?''

Joanna blushed and was glad of the cover of darkness.

"We met last fall at a writer's conference. She spends her summers here, too. The weekends, anyway. The rest of the time, she's in New York running the publishing industry— or just about.''

Joanna stared into the flames with oddly turbulent feelings. "So, this Joyce of yours—she's actually sold your novel for you?''

"Yes, to Gateway Books, and finagled a sizable advance for me, too, even though the thing's not even done yet.''

"Oh, Michael, that's wonderful!"

"Not wonderful. But it'll tide me over till royalties come in—or I sell something else."

"I guess Casey and I really threw a monkey wrench into your plans, showing up out of the blue. I'm sorry."

He tossed a hand dismissively, though she noticed he didn't deny it. "Things'll work out."

"When do you expect this novel to be on the market?"

"In about a year, if I ever get around to finishing it."

"I'm sure you will."

"Sure." He fell into reflective silence. "But will it be as good as if I had unlimited time?" Joanna was pierced by the depth of concern in his eyes. "Jo, I *am* a good writer, and this novel—all my instincts tell me..." He looked away in sudden embarrassment.

"...that it's right on target?"

"Yes. Oh, yes!" Joanna couldn't help hearing the breathlessness in his voice. "I just want the whole thing to be good, beginning to end. But these last few chapters... I hate having a gun to my head." He paused. "I sometimes get these crazy visions of a roomful of editors reading the last chapters and keeling over with laughter."

"Fat chance! If they bought your book just on the strength of the first few chapters..."

"Joyce says that, too," he interrupted a little too eagerly. Joanna could feel her own enthusiasm momentarily flicker. "If you listen to her, I'm going to be rich and famous within a year."

"Since when does Michael Malone have such doubts about himself?"

"Oh, I don't have any about *myself*. I wouldn't have quit the university if I did. It's just that I've been publishing for years—poetry, short stories, essays. This isn't even my first novel."

"It isn't?"

"No. My first wasn't so bad, either. It even got into print, but it didn't go anywhere. I didn't know Joyce at the time."

Joanna forced a smile. "So, you expected to be rich and famous overnight? You were just paying your dues, that's all."

"Actually I never expected to be rich and famous at all. I just wanted to be good. But now..." He shuddered and laughed as if the idea frightened and amazed him all at the same time.

"You must be very happy."

"Yes. Yes." His vision seemed to turn inward. "But there are times...well, it could be better."

"What do you mean? How much better can it get?"

"Well...look at me! Here I am nearly thirty, and I no longer have the security of a regular job. I don't have a home. I don't have a wife, kids, a dog. You name it, and I don't have it! I feel sort of like a boat without a rudder."

Joanna chuckled. "Oh, really! Tell me about it!"

"You, too?" Again that tentative smile. Joanna felt her heart jump. A companionable warmth had stolen over her while Michael had been talking and although she didn't know how or why, his revelations had dispelled her own stubborn refusal to talk.

"Becoming a widow is pretty much the same. All of a sudden, all my reasons for being who I was and doing the things I did vanished. Without Phil, I have to build a whole new life for myself. Of course, there's still Casey." She closed her fist as if hanging on to an invisible lifeline.

"And you still have your job."

"Y-yes. But it's not like a career I chose on my own. I went to work there only because it was a family business and our apartment was right upstairs."

"Oh, I see." Mist was thickening the air now, and Michael's hair was beaded with tiny silver droplets of moisture.

"I don't think I want to keep that apartment much longer, either. There are too many memories there. It's not doing Casey any good."

Michael's attention intensified. "I thought not."

"It really worries me, Michael."

"Give him time."

She nodded. "That's why I brought him to the Vineyard. He...we both needed to get away." Even if talking didn't actually solve anything, she felt so much better having Michael there to hear her out.

"Lately I've been thinking about looking for another job, too...or maybe going back to school, getting a degree."

"Great!"

"No, not great. It'll be an expense I can't afford. And I'll hardly ever see Casey. But maybe with a degree I'll be able to find a job that will allow me and Casey to live a little better."

Michael's face grew grim. "I guess I've never thought of you as head of a household before. Has it been rough, Jo?"

"We've managed," she tossed off, then made the mistake of looking into his eyes. "All right, at times it's been rough."

"What are you planning to study if you go back to school?"

"I don't know. Computer Science?"

His look sharpened and went right through her. If ever there was a touchstone in her life, it was Michael.

"I have to think of the present job market," she said defensively.

"I haven't said a word!"

"Yeah, sure, but I know what you're thinking. You're thinking I always hated math. But we all can't be as idealistic as you and write novels, Michael. Some of us have to compromise." At that moment, she felt so lost that her lips quivered. "Actually I don't know *what* I'm doing. My life is just so gray and fractured right now. And that's why *I* need the cottage so badly this summer. I really need to rest, think clearly, find out what I'd like to do with the rest of my life." The immensity of her statement made her groan. She dropped her head to her knees and shook it from side to side.

Across the fire, Michael laughed quietly. "Aren't we a pair, though!"

She lifted her eyes. "A couple of champs." And they both laughed.

"I think what we need is a stiff cup of coffee," she said. "Do you have any?"

"That's the first thing I packed." She crept into the tent and took the thermos out of the picnic basket. Back at the fire, she poured out two cups. When she handed one to Michael, their fingers brushed. Their eyes met nervously.

"Michael?"

"Hmm?"

"I'm sorry about last night, too. I said a lot of things that were unfair, but my anger was leading the way. I seem to have had a whole lot of that stored up inside me."

"It's all right. I came out here offering an apology, not looking for one." He sipped his hot coffee pensively, and she knew he was thinking about the previous night again, as she was.

"I really am sorry," she said. "I hope you don't have any bumps or bruises from that fall."

"No. Not from the fall." He sipped his coffee and stared into the fire. Then, probably knowing that she was staring back with deepening curiosity, he slowly lifted the hem of his jeans.

Joanna bit her lip.

"Barbarian!" he whispered.

Joanna's gaze lifted from the raw scrape on his shin to his face and realized he was trying to suppress a smile.

"That was a pretty stupid move...."

"The whole argument was. Idiotic!"

Suddenly they both began to laugh, releasing whatever tension still lingered between them over the incident last night.

Michael set down his coffee mug and stood, looking like a huge idol in the distorted shadows thrown by the fire. "As long as we've managed to strike this truce... I'll be right back. Don't go away."

Joanna watched him clamber over the dune and disappear into the darkness. But within a minute he was back, a sleeping bag riding on his shoulder. He swung it to the sand and reseated himself.

"Actually the real reason I came out here was I didn't like the idea of you two camping out all alone."

"Oh, and did you come to protect us?"

He grinned endearingly. "Sort of. You don't mind, do you? I haven't done any camping in years."

She shrugged. "It's a big beach."

"Yeah, you *would* make me sleep out on a night like tonight."

"You should've brought a tent. The weatherman says it might even rain."

"Very funny." He picked up his mug and drained its contents. They became quiet, and their silence gradually deepened into private thoughts.

"Jo, I feel like a total heel for not having extended my condolences to you yet, and well, you must know how sorry I feel about your loss."

"Yes, of course."

"I know Phil's illness was a burden—your father kept me informed—and you probably don't need me dredging it all up again, but I want you to know I thought about you a lot and prayed for you to have courage." His voice was hushed now, and at times Joanna confused it with the plaintive sighing of the wind.

"Thank you. That means a lot to me. But I wish you could have been upset about Phil's dying instead of my having to cope with it."

"Sorry, but I didn't know him, except for the little you told me. Was . . . was he good to you, Jo?"

"Yes. A good father to Casey, too."

"Good. I'm glad you were happy." The corners of his mouth drooped strangely. "Bunny and I were never happy." The driftwood crackled and broke, sending up a yellow spiral of sparks. For a while, the whole world seemed consumed by its heat.

"You don't have to tell me about your marriage."

"But I want to. I feel like talking. In fact, talk is just what you and I seem to need most right now. I just can't go on letting you believe that fairy tale I told you the other night, all that nonsense about Bunny loving our life together. She hated it. We fought constantly about how little money I made and about my writing. She actually used to laugh when I said I wanted to be a writer. What she wanted me to do was quit grad school and join her father's brokerage firm in Boston."

"Michael, please!" Joanna closed her eyes. "You shouldn't talk about her. It's like spreading gossip about the dead."

"But it's the one thing we *have* to talk about. We've stored up too much anger for too long, and we both know what's at the bottom of it."

"No!" she snapped decisively. "I don't want to hear it."

Dismay sank furrows into Michael's handsome face. "You're probably right." He seemed deflated, but Joanna didn't care. She didn't want to hear about his marriage. As comfortable as she'd begun to feel with him, there was still a proud little voice within her that made her pull back. She didn't want to be appeased with tales of how unhappy he had been with Bunny. She didn't want excuses now. Nothing could amend the fact that he had coldly, deliberately lied to her, used her, and then dumped her for Bunny.

The night suddenly seemed to grow damp and cold, as if the wind had stirred the warm spell of the fire and spiraled it away.

"Maybe we should call it a night," she suggested, and before Michael could protest, she got to her feet.

Inside the tent, she crawled into her bag and snuggled down, searching for some warmth. Casey was still sleeping soundly. Outside, she could hear the rip of a cord and the flop of a bedroll hitting sand. Suddenly Joanna felt awful. Michael was camping out at the foot of their tent like a sentry at a castle gate. He was too worried to leave them alone; he had apologized for last night, initiated a truce—

and she was indeed feeling better for it—and now she was making him sleep out on a raw, misty night.

"Psst! There's room in here," she called.

A moment later, Michael was in the tent, carefully spreading his sleeping bag on the other side of Casey. "I'm usually not this much of a pushover. I usually play hard-to-get, especially on a first date, but under the circumstances . . . just promise you'll respect me in the morning."

Joanna felt a smile tugging at her tightly pressed lips. He had always been able to do that, no matter how dark her mood.

"Hush up and get settled. Lord! You're as graceful as a rhinoceros!"

"Ahh," he finally sighed. "Heaven!"

Outside, the wind buffeted the sand and flung it like rain against the tent. There was barely a glimmer of light now from the fire, but she could still make out Michael's eyes fixed on her over Casey's small body.

"Jo, I don't want you coming out here just to avoid me." She tried to protest, but he reached over and put a finger on her lips. "Shh. I saw your bags, too. You were planning to leave, weren't you? I don't blame you. I said some pretty nasty things last night, and I'm sorry. And for all it's worth, I'm glad you didn't leave. The house feels empty without you." His voice died on a whisper, but it took Joanna's breath away.

She turned and stared at the canvas peak overhead, not knowing why there was such a tightness in her throat.

"Jo, I have to keep on talking. Somehow we've connected tonight, and knowing how proud and stubborn we can both get, this moment may never come again."

Joanna swallowed with difficulty, her throat so hard and dry it ached.

"Jo, what I was trying to tell you before...I never loved Bunny. Our marriage was a farce."

His words pressed down on her, stopping the breath in her lungs. So, what did he expect her to say in answer? She rolled over with her face to the wall. A tear trickled from her eye over the bridge of her nose.

"Jo," he whispered. His voice sounded as if he were desperately trying to keep in touch with someone slipping away into the sky. "Jo, I married Bunny because she said she was pregnant, and I was too young to fight all the people telling me what I was supposed to do—Bunny's father, that crazy Wilcox woman, my mother, even your father. I was hemmed in.

"But that didn't matter to me. Even if they'd doubled their pressure, I wouldn't have married Bunny if you hadn't run off and left me the way you did." He paused and Joanna thought she heard his breath catch on a sob. "But in the end, I married Bunny because you went home and married Phil. I didn't have anything left to live for.

"What I still don't understand is why you married Phil. *Was* it because you'd planned to all along? Or…or did you marry him on the rebound? I've lived with speculation for so long I don't know what to think anymore. Didn't you love me, Jo? Weren't we so crazy in love with each other we couldn't see straight? Or did I dream the whole thing up?"

Joanna's pulse was pumping so hard her temples hurt. She was rigid with terror. Perspiration broke out on her face.

"Jo," he called insistently. "Why did you marry Phil?"

His question pressed on her like a gigantic boulder, crushing her bones. There was no way she could answer—no way she *would* answer. It was too late. The lie had gone on too long. And so she didn't.

The silence in the tent became oppressive. The question hung there unanswered until he must have finally thought she'd gone to sleep. She heard him sigh with resignation and, a moment later, roll over, too.

CHAPTER EIGHT

JOANNA WOKE to a damp, chilly dawn. She turned her head and looked at Michael and Casey, still asleep in the thin gray light. Unexpectedly her heart swelled with emotion. For once, she stopped fighting herself and admitted that it felt good to be with Michael again. It was a joy to wake up and realize he was there, not hundreds of miles away. To know she'd have the chance to talk to him today, see his face, his eyes, his smile, hear his deep, soul-moving voice.

Michael's long black lashes fluttered and he opened his eyes. "Good morning," he whispered.

She smiled peacefully, her gaze linked with his. They said nothing for a while, just listened to the wind gusting over the beach. Joanna had thought sleep would elude her. For a long time, she'd lain awake, face to the tent's wall, turning over Michael's words in her heart. She had tried to make sense of them, but it had been like trying to put together a puzzle with too many pieces missing.

Had he really loved her as much as he'd said? It was possible. But her thoughts had invariably come back to the same dead end. If he had loved her so much, how could he have been seeing Bunny at the same time? And he must have been for Bunny to be pregnant.

He'd also said he never would have married Bunny if she hadn't married Phil. Well, she hadn't married Phil for four weeks. In the meantime, why hadn't Michael tried to contact her? If he'd loved her so much, why hadn't he even called? And what about his responsibilities to Bunny and to their unborn child?

There were lies snaking through his story everywhere, and she'd be a fool to think he was doing anything but rationalizing his way out of a bad conscience.

Joanna had finally fallen asleep, weary with unanswered questions. Unanswered? They'd never been asked. Michael had wanted to talk. Maybe if she had simply asked...but she had turned her back on him, pretended to be asleep. She had deliberately blocked all channels of communication. But she'd felt so panicked at the time, she hadn't known what else to do.

It was quiet now, peaceful. Maybe the issue could be broached again.

"Joanna?" He spoke before she could frame the right words.

"Yes?" She searched his face expectantly.

"About our conversation last night..." He rolled onto his back, releasing himself from her gaze. "I'm sorry if I probed where I shouldn't have. I've had the night to think about it, and I guess you were right. It was inappropriate to talk about Bunny the way I did, and I had no business asking you about Phil. Maybe some things *are* best left in the past. I thought it might straighten out some misunderstandings if we talked, that maybe we could relax around each other a little more if we cleared the air. But obviously you feel better letting sleeping dogs lie. Fine. I guess it doesn't make any difference anymore. It's all over and done with—water over the dam, so to speak. No amount of talk is going to change it. Right?"

Joanna swallowed with difficulty. "Right," she whispered, staring at his finely chiseled profile. All of it, water over the dam.

"All right then. I won't bring up the subject again. Only..." He turned, his long black lashes shading his eyes. "Let's put an end to the sniping, Jo. We both desperately need a summer of peace."

"Yes, let's, *please*."

He reached across Casey and gently tucked a strand of her hair behind her ear. As his fingers lingered on her cheek, Joanna became aware of a pleasurable warmth stealing over her. It puzzled and dismayed her, and she was relieved when he drew away.

"I know things aren't completely right between us, and maybe they never will be, but as I said, maybe it doesn't matter. We can still call a truce and go on from here, share the house amicably..."

"Or at least without murdering each other."

"Oh, I hope so," he laughed. "Maybe we can even learn how to be friends again. We were great friends at one time, weren't we?"

Joanna eased onto her back and closed her eyes, remembering. "I'll stay at the cottage. I'll try not to snipe. But we're both carrying too much emotional baggage to delude ourselves into thinking we can promise more."

Michael's lips worked wordlessly. "I know," he finally said.

Suddenly there was an ominous tapping on the canvas overhead. They were both silent, listening. Within seconds, rain was pelting the roof with a deafening beat.

"Oh, no!" Joanna groaned. "Michael, it's raining!"

"No kidding."

"What are we going to do?"

"I haven't the foggiest. Think we're here for the duration?"

"Oh, Lord!"

"How much food did you bring?"

"Just enough for breakfast, but—"

"Hey! What...you...Uncle Michael!" Casey cried out.

"Morning, kid." Michael smiled.

"How did you get here?" the child asked excitedly. "Hey, it's raining. Ugh! It's all wet under me! I didn't do it, Ma, honest!"

Joanna laughed at his energetic flow of chatter. Much to her surprise, Michael was laughing, too.

"How do kids wake up so fast?" he said. "I usually need two cups of coffee before I can gear myself up to that kind of enthusiasm."

Casey crawled out of his sleeping bag and before either adult could stop him, undid the door flap. A shower of rain came gusting in. They all screamed, and Michael scrambled to his knees to zip up the opening again. Joanna expected him to be a angry—or at least a little miffed—but she was wrong.

"Isn't this fun!" he cheered. "Let's have some breakfast."

"Are you crazy?" Joanna laughed, amazed at how quickly the mood in the tent had changed.

"No, just famished. What do you have that's edible?"

"Bananas."

"Oh, boy, Casey! Bananas!" At that moment, a drop of water plinked him on his unshaven cheek. Everyone looked up and noticed the stain of moisture spreading across the canvas over his head. *Plink!* Another drop hit his eye. In the distance, thunder grumbled angrily.

Unexpectedly, a giggle rippled up through Joanna's ribs. How absurd they were, caught in a thunderstorm, in a tiny, leaky tent, a mile's walk from the cottage! How utterly absurd! She fell back and laughed harder.

Michael tried to ignore the rain now dripping rapidly on his head and asked with dignified calm, "What, may I inquire, are you laughing at?"

Joanna couldn't answer. All she could do was point.

"Laughing at me?" he said with affronted innocence, all the while reaching stealthily into the picnic basket. A second later, he was wielding a large banana and flogging her around the shoulders with it.

"Stop! Stop it!" Joanna cried, laughing raggedly. She grabbed up her knapsack and swung it at his head.

Casey caught the silly mood of the two adults and jumped to his feet, looking for a weapon of his own.

"No, Case..." Joanna cried in alarm, but too late. Suddenly the roof of the small tent came folding in and the walls buckled.

"Do you suppose we'll ever learn to do anything right, Joanna?" Michael's muffled voice drawled from somewhere under the toppled mess.

They finally made it back to the cottage, cold, drenched and gritty with sand. But they were exhilarated. It was as if they'd been on a great adventure and were dying to tell someone about it.

Their good mood persisted throughout the rainy morning, too, although it later sprang from a sense of well-being derived from a steaming shower, dry clothes and a cup of rich, hot chocolate.

Joanna was curled up on the couch, sipping from her mug, while Michael and Casey adjusted the logs on the fire.

"There, that ought to break the chill." Michael gazed at the crackling fire. "Keep the mildew down, too."

"Ma, can I watch TV?"

"Sure, *Sesame Street* will be on in a few minutes."

Michael clapped ashes off his hands. "*Sesame Street*. You know, I've never seen that show. Heard a lot about it, though."

Joanna pinned him with a look not unlike the one she usually reserved for Casey when he was trying to squirm out of a chore. "Don't you have some work to do?"

Michael dug his hands into his pockets and nodded boyishly.

"Well?"

He sighed. "I'm going. I'm going."

Joanna liked this new atmosphere of calm. It sure beat what they'd lived with before. Everyone seemed so much more at ease. And yet she couldn't help thinking it was a fragile calm and that it didn't run all that deep. True, they had dispelled a lot of their anger the other night, but she couldn't help fearing that they were merely floating on the surface, pretending the water beneath them wasn't still deep and perilously dark.

EARLY THE NEXT MORNING, Joanna got a call from Nathan. He had just stopped by his sister's on his way to work, and Meg had reminded him of a concert they'd bought tickets for months ago.

"It's this weekend. Would you like to go?"

Joanna hesitated. Nathan had taken her out to dinner Monday night, out on the boat Tuesday, and here it was just Thursday and he was asking her out again. Was Michael right about Nathan still carrying a torch for her? At the time, she'd thought he was just clutching at straws to start an argument.

"Can I let you know tomorrow?" She cringed as he waited for a reason and she came up with none.

Finally, "Sure, no problem. I'll call again tomorrow. Oh, before I go, my sister would like to talk to you."

Meg came on the line then and asked Joanna what plans she'd made for the day.

"Well, I've been dying to get into Edgartown, do some browsing, shopping..."

"Great. How about doing me a favor and bringing your son over here? He and Paul played so well the other day I hardly knew they were around."

Joanna considered the proposal. No matter how Meg phrased it, she knew Meg was doing her the favor. "All right. But one of these days, I'm going to have to reciprocate."

Joanna spent an enjoyable morning wandering through shops and strolling the streets of Edgartown. It was a lovely, warm morning, the air fresh and sunny after the previous day's storm.

Though Edgartown had been settled in 1642, it really hadn't flourished until the mid 1800s. Those were the golden years of whaling, and the streets facing the harbor were lined with the stately homes built by the money that had flowed in. Driving by, you simply could not appreciate their beauty. You had to walk, stop, admire their elaborately fanlighted doorways, their prim fences spilling over with roses, the widows' walks crowning their peaks. And Joanna did just that, snapping nearly two rolls of film in the process.

By early afternoon, however, she was anxious to leave. Meg had offered to give Casey lunch, but Joanna didn't want to take advantage of her hospitality.

"Meg?" she called through the kitchen screen door. "Will you tell Casey I'm back?"

"He isn't here, Jo." Meg turned from the counter where she was rinsing dishes. "Come on in."

"What? Where is he?"

"With Michael."

"Michael!"

"Yeah, you know, that guy with the deep sexy voice and bedroom eyes who lives at your place," she mocked laughingly. "He came by for Casey at least half an hour ago...said something about going fishing."

Joanna's green eyes widened with confusion. "Where'd they go?"

"Down to the pond, I think."

"Thanks."

"Hey, don't you want to stay for some iced tea?"

But Joanna was already in her car.

She could see them even before she reached the cottage. They were sitting at the end of the dock, legs dangling over the side. On their heads, to protect them from the sun, were identical sailor hats of light blue poplin—Vivien's and her father's.

Joanna jumped out of her car and ran across the yard. She didn't understand her sudden mood, but she was both frightened and angry. What did Michael think he was doing? She didn't mind the fact that under the new truce he had become quite civil around the house, but she'd never asked him to go this far.

An irrational possessiveness filled her. She was desperate to rescue Casey from a harm she could not name but genuinely felt, when something made her pause. A laugh. Casey's laugh. In spite of her anger, Joanna started to watch them.

It was nothing short of a calendar picture—a boy and a man, sitting at the end of an old wooden dock, their lines bobbing lazily on a blue, rippled pond. It was a scene straight out of Norman Rockwell. *Summer Idyll* it should be called.

Then she noticed something else, something amazing considering the difference in their ages. It was the similarity in the lines of their shoulders, in the long stretch of their backs. Casey not only had hair the same texture as Michael's and eyes the same dark blue, but he was going to grow up to have his build, too.

At that moment, Michael leaned over and in spite of the distance, Joanna heard Casey's laugh again. Unexpectedly her eyes filled with tears, and the summer idyll blurred and swam out of focus. It took her well over five minutes to compose herself.

"Damn you!" she cursed, wiping her cheeks with the back of her hand. By the time she set foot on the dock, every trace of sentimentality was gone from her face.

"Michael, you could have let a person know about this!" She walked down the dock with brisk, aggressive strides, her soft, flowered dress swinging around her knees.

Michael turned calmly and squinted up at her from under the brim of his hat. How blue his eyes were, here by the water and open sky! How much depth of character was added by the small creases fanning out from their corners! For a moment, Joanna's heart skipped a treacherously quick beat. Her fear deepened.

"What's that?" he asked languorously.

Casey turned, too. The brim of his hat had been secured with a safety pin to clear his eyes. "Ma, I caught a fish!" he cried exultantly, scrambling to his feet.

"Really?" For her son's sake, she momentarily set aside her emotions.

"Uh huh." He nodded vigorously and his hat fell forward.

"Let me hold your pole, Case," Michael offered.

With his hands freed, Casey lifted a heavy bucket. "See?"

Joanna peered down at a small silvery fish, one eye coolly staring back at her. "Very good!" she laughed. But when her eyes linked with Michael's, her smile dropped again.

He gave Casey back his pole, propped his own against a piling, and stood up. Then he and Joanna moved out of Casey's earshot.

"I'm sorry if I've put you out," he said. "But I didn't think Casey would mind getting out of that house. It's full of strangers and noisy as hell and—"

"Don't make excuses," she whispered with a vehemence she didn't intend. "I just drove miles out of my way but you did nothing wrong. You didn't even—"

"What did you want me to do?"

"You could have let me know!"

"How? Mental telepathy? I didn't get the idea till after you were gone." He was leaning so close Joanna could feel the heat of his body and smell the clean, spicy fragrance of his after-shave. His closeness was oddly disturbing.

"In any case, what harm's been done? What's the big deal?"

"Well...well, there are all sorts of things to consider." Her eyes darted across the landscape searching for something, anything. "You can't just take a five-year-old fishing without preparation. For instance, have you bothered to put sunscreen on him?"

"Joanna, the boy's skin is browner than mine!" he retorted, his blue eyes beginning to flash.

"Did he go to the bathroom before he left Meg's?"

"Guys don't have to worry about such things. Besides, the cottage is just up the hill."

"Well...do you realize it's nearly two? I always give Casey a snack in the afternoon. Have you packed a snack? And what if I'd already made plans for him? How would I drag him off this dock now after you've...after you've..."

"What is it, Jo? What's really bugging you? So far, I haven't heard a single protest that holds water."

She was speechless, devoid of answers, knowing only that some instinctive fear was driving her to act this way.

"And I actually thought I was doing you a favor bringing him fishing. I do have more important things to tend to, you know."

"Well, why don't you go do them and leave us alone?" Her tone was unintentionally caustic. Michael's mood had changed, too. She could see it in the tightening of his jaw.

"What is it, Jo?"

"Nothing," she answered sullenly.

"I don't believe it. You just don't like me spending time with him. That's it, isn't it?"

"Yes. No! I mean..." Joanna bit her lip, suddenly realizing that he was right.

Michael nodded self-righteously. "Sure. I can see it in your eyes. In spite of everything you say to the contrary, you're determined to keep that boy aware of his father's memory. You're so determined that you can't stand the idea of his spending even one afternoon with another adult male."

Joanna was stunned by his misinterpretation of her motives. "No! That's not it at all!" But he wasn't listening.

"Can't you see how futile it is?" Michael went on. "It's downright stupid, too. It'll do more harm than you think. The boy needs men in his life."

"Oh? And what makes you such an authority on child rearing?"

"It's just common sense."

"Michael, do us all a favor and stop inventing problems he doesn't have."

"He *will* have them if you keep isolating him."

"I'm not isolating him!" Joanna spat defensively. "We've managed quite well so far without your sage advice, and I'm sure we'll manage in the future."

"Yeah," he drawled, "I don't know why I should even give a damn."

"You? Give a damn? Michael, until yesterday you barely said two words to the boy. You'd think he was carrying some contagious disease or something."

"That's not true."

"It is, too! What's wrong, Michael? What is it about Casey you don't like? Is it the fact that your son died and Casey lived? Do you resent him because he's the same age yours would have been? Does he remind you of what you lost?"

This time it was Michael's turn to be stunned. His face suffused with dark color. "Where did you ever dig up such a stupid notion?" he whispered incredulously.

Joanna immediately felt tactless as she studied his reaction. How callous could she be?

"If I kept my distance from Casey, and I admit I did at first, it was only because he was a living, breathing reminder that you deserted me to marry somebody else. You had this child with someone else, you had this life I wasn't a part of..." His voice rasped with emotion. "I certainly don't resent Casey, Joanna. I think he's a terrific little guy. I only resent myself for being such a damn fool when I was young. Now, if you'll excuse me..." He started to move away, but Joanna clutched his arm. Her fingers tingled as they came in contact with the warm, hair-coarsened skin.

"Then it had nothing to do with Bunny's miscarriage?"

Michael thrust his hand through his thick, unruly hair and squinted out over the water. "There was no miscarriage," he said bitterly.

Joanna blinked confusedly. "W-what?"

"Look, Joanna, I thought you wanted to leave all this in the past. I thought we weren't going to bring it up again."

"But how can I just...*what* did you say?"

He turned to her, an empty sadness in his eyes. "There was no miscarriage. Bunny pretended to have one. She came out of the bathroom crying and weak, but when I took her to the hospital—against her wishes, I might add—

the doctor who examined her said she was fine. In fact, she'd never even been pregnant.''

Joanna felt herself swooning. "But... your mother told me she went for tests..."

"Bunny said she did. Her parents believed her, and without anyone bothering to confirm it, it became an accepted fact."

"Then there was no pregnancy?"

"How many ways do you want me to admit it?" he said icily. "Does it amuse you to hear I got duped—me, the guy you thought was such a hotshot with women! Are you glad I got caught and was made to pay for my sins?"

Joanna stared at him for a few long seconds. Then, slowly, she pulled herself out of her shock. "No, I don't find it amusing, and I'm definitely not glad." How could he even think such a thing? She felt only sadness and an incredible frustration. All that unhappiness... all those years lost to them! And all because of a lie! Joanna was so overwhelmed with sadness she couldn't even be angry at Bunny.

"She must have really loved you to make up a story like that and to suffer the embarrassment of gossip—just to get you to marry her."

"You call that love, trapping an innocent person?"

"Innocent?"

"That's right." He spun away and glared out over the water.

"Michael, what are you trying to say?"

"Forget it, Jo." Under his knit shirt, his shoulder muscles tensed.

She lifted her hand to touch him but instantly thought better of it. "Well, I'm sorry you had to go through that. It must have been awful." He wouldn't look at her, and she didn't blame him. She wasn't getting across even a fraction of what was in her heart.

There was obviously no place to go with this conversation, and she didn't try. "Better get back to your fishing.

Bring Casey up to the house—whenever," she finished vaguely.

He nodded and she left him standing there on the dock, his chin lifted proudly. But she noticed a decided slump in his usual confident stance.

CHAPTER NINE

JOANNA WAS SORRY she'd been so harsh with Michael. He obviously had more pain in his past than she'd ever imagined. Besides, he wasn't going to do her son any harm, not if she was careful. The summer was too short. She should have controlled those defensive feelings before she'd gone out on the dock and acted so irrationally. She had upset the companionable mood they'd recently fallen into, and she deeply regretted it. She returned to the cottage determined to set things right.

By the time Michael and Casey came up from the dock, she had made a potato salad, baked a chocolate cake, and prepared the grill for hamburgers. She was quickly coming to the conclusion that cooking separate meals was ridiculous, as ridiculous as trying to divide the air each of them breathed. So much wasted energy! Besides, she'd noticed that Michael was usually too busy to cook and didn't eat well. And though she tried not to think too much about it, that worried her.

Michael looked at the cheerful yellow plates set out on the picnic table. Then he looked at Joanna, poking the hot coals with a long-handled fork. She had changed out of her dress into a bright pink halter and matching satin running shorts. She knew she looked far more rested than when she'd arrived, and her skin was now a healthy gold. What she didn't expect was the sudden headiness she felt when Michael's eyes registered the fact.

"And what are we supposed to do with all these fish?" he asked, setting down the pail. He stood with legs aggressively apart, one fist on his hip, the other gripping a pole.

Casey peeked up at him and struck the same pose. Joanna looked from one to the other and laughed. If she didn't, she was afraid she might cry.

"We'll have them tomorrow," she said. "Let's go put them on ice and wash our hands. Boy, what a catch!"

On Friday morning, Nathan called again. He was at his Edgartown store. Having come up with no believable excuse overnight, Joanna agreed to go with him to the concert Saturday night, chiding herself for being so reluctant in the first place.

Then, to provide a morning of undisturbed quiet for Michael, she took Casey out to Gay Head. When they came back, hours later, Michael was still at the typewriter.

"Are you still working?" Joanna asked, peeking into his room. He turned stiffly.

"Uncle Michael!" Casey burst into the room. "I talked to a Indian!"

Michael's tired eyes crinkled as the boy ran up to him. "'A Indian'?"

Casey scrambled into his lap. "At Gay Head. They live there."

"Is that where you got this?" Michael lifted an intricately beaded necklace from the boy's chest.

"Uh huh. They were selling them. I got these, too." He spread out a fistful of postcards on Michael's manuscript—colorful pictures of the Gay Head lighthouse, the steep clay cliffs, a family of Wampanoag Indians, the Menemsha fishing village at sunset.

"On the way back we saw a mother turkey, too."

Michael shot Joanna a quizzical look.

"A wild turkey. I couldn't believe it. I thought those things were extinct. She was just walking along the side of the road with a couple of chicks, so I stopped the car and got out to get a better look."

"But it chased Mommy," Casey finished for her, laughing merrily behind his hand.

"Damn thing scared me half to death!" Michael laughed, too, she was glad to notice.

"Sounds like you had quite a morning."

"We did. And you?"

"I got a lot written, but I sure could use a break. Anyone here feel like going for a swim?"

Casey slid off his lap and did a little dance across the rug. Joanna couldn't help laughing. She hadn't seen him so happy in months.

Her bathing suit was a simple black maillot with a deep, plunging neckline and high, cutaway legs. It made her legs look twice as long and revealed the entire inner swell of her bosom. She felt self-conscious wearing it and wished she hadn't bought it, but at the time it had seemed such a bargain.

Standing on the dock, she unzipped her terry robe with grave reluctance. Michael, who was buckling an orange life jacket around Casey, looked up from where he was kneeling. Instantly she yearned to pull the robe back on. His eyes held a glitter she knew only too well.

"Wow! Look at your mother in that suit!" he said, leaning conspiratorially close to the child. Casey cupped a hand over his mouth and giggled. "Mothers aren't supposed to look like that. How come yours does?"

Joanna felt her face flush. She suspected Michael was just making fun of her and tried to look unruffled. She dug into her canvas carryall for a brush and proceeded to tie her hair back into a ponytail. Then, still feeling his eyes on her, she walked to the edge of the dock. She wanted to leap off immediately and conceal herself in the water, but suddenly an unexpected playfulness overtook her shyness. She looked over her shoulder with a confident smile. "If you've got it, flaunt it!" she said, wiggling her bottom. Then she jumped off the dock, none too gracefully, she had to admit. The cold water rushed over her ears, drowning out Michael's deep, raucous laugh.

It was a hot afternoon and the water felt glorious. For over two hours, they swam and dived and played a game of water tag. Too often, however, Joanna found herself just treading water beside Michael, talking about inconsequential matters. Too often his hand came drifting to her waist to keep her afloat. Too often she felt the cool brush of their legs.

How it reminded her of that other summer, when Michael would touch her that way and the touch would be too much too handle! He would pull her into his arms and cover her mouth with his and in his reckless passion invariably take her under, coming up only when it seemed they might drown. There was a soft humor in Michael's eyes that made her wonder if he was remembering those days, too.

When they'd finally had enough, Michael hoisted Casey onto the dock. Then he leaned over to give Joanna his hand. As she swung up, his arm wrapped around her waist to steady her balance. But his hold on her lingered a moment too long, and she felt the hardness of his wet thigh pressed against hers.

She went weak so quickly she didn't have time to halt her reaction. She leaned closer, and the hand that had unthinkingly come to rest on his chest became alive and aware of the flesh beneath it. A wave of heat coursed through her, and from the serious expression around Michael's mouth, she was sure he felt it, too.

They moved apart abruptly. Joanna scooped up a towel and rubbed it briskly over her burning skin.

They walked back up the path talking as if nothing had happened, and perhaps, she thought, nothing had. Her imagination had just run wild. Certainly, after all the resentment and hurt they'd carried around for so long, there couldn't still be any physical attraction left! Could there?

Instead of dwelling on it, she turned her attention to the fragrant tangle of bayberry and honeysuckle along the path. The bushes were humming with summer insects. Overhead, a wheel of gulls cawed loudly against a cloudless blue sky. The smell of marsh grass rode the air, and all up and down her arms and legs was the tickle of salt water drying. Joanna took a deep breath and smiled. It had been years since she'd felt so alive, so sensually aware of her surroundings.

They decided to make a supper of the previous day's catch. But first the fish had to be cleaned. With Casey watching intently from the end of the picnic table, she and Michael scaled and cut. As they worked, she noticed that they laughed a lot—giddily, comfortably, as tired people often do.

Just as they were finishing up, however, there was the sound of a car door slamming in the front yard.

"Oh, no! Look at me!" Joanna cried with a nervous giggle. Her still-damp hair was matted and snarled from swimming. Innumerable silver scales dotted her arms and legs, and her terry robe was soiled where she had been wiping her hands.

Michael strode off to the side yard and broke into a smile. He waved casually, and suddenly Joanna felt a shadow of dread falling over her good mood.

A moment later, the visitor appeared—a tall brunette in high-heeled sandals and a smart, perfectly crisp dress of cool navy-blue. Every strand of her long, luxuriant hair was in place, not a millimeter of her nail polish chipped.

The feeling of dread deepened as Joanna watched her and Michael embrace... the familiar fit of her arm around Michael's neck, the casual kiss on the cheek as if she were confident there would be time enough later for deeper intimacies.

"Jo, I'd like you to meet Joyce Sterling," Michael said with what Joanna thought was a bit too much pride. "Joyce, this is Joanna."

Joanna made a hasty pass at her robe and shook the woman's hand. So this was Joyce Sterling, Michael's high-powered literary agent. She should have known. Joanna guessed Joyce to be in her mid- to late-thirties, but her age was hardly a liability. In fact, Joyce's age only added a dimension of mature intelligence and cosmopolitan sophistication to her already obvious assets.

"Nice to meet you, Joanna," Joyce said, her keen dark eyes quickly sweeping Joanna from head to feet. She smiled.

Joanna smiled back, warmly she hoped. Bunny had been attractive in much the same way, she remembered—tall and cool, with a sense of style that had left Joanna feeling cloddish by comparison. Joyce should come as no surprise. What did surprise Joanna were the growing knots of hostility she thought she'd outgrown along with her braces.

"I didn't even know Michael had a sister till he told me about you last Saturday night."

They had talked about her last weekend? "Oh...I'm not his sister."

"Excuse me. Stepsister."

Yes, whatever. It obviously didn't matter.

"I hope I'm not disturbing anything," Joyce continued, her voice a deep, melodic lilt. "I should have called."

"Don't be silly." Michael swung a lawn chair around and invited her to sit. "You're not disturbing a thing."

Only the best time you and I have shared in six years, Joanna thought peevishly.

Michael glanced at his watch.

"I left New York early," Joyce explained, reading his gesture. "I thought I'd beat the weekend traffic at the airport." Her dark eyes were fixed on Joanna's legs now, at the scales clinging as tenaciously as barnacles, at the dirt shading her toes.

"If you'll excuse me, I'd better take this fish inside." Joanna gathered up the food and utensils and took them into the house. She slung the fish into the refrigerator and dropped the rest of her burden into the sink. Then she ran upstairs, tearing off her grimy robe as she went. She drew a hasty washcloth over her arms and legs and brushed out her tangled hair. Then she slipped a long shirt over her swimsuit.

Michael was sitting next to Joyce when she got back downstairs. His arm lightly draped the back of her chair. Casey was standing in front of them, regaling Joyce with his fishing adventure of the previous day. Joanna paused at the sun porch door to listen.

Joyce's dark head turned, eyes glittering with a hard luster. "So, you went fishing, huh?" she teased Michael, though Joanna sensed an undercurrent of reprimand.

"And we went swimming today," Casey boasted. "All afternoon!"

Joanna could have sworn the woman's nostrils flared.

"Don't sweat it, Joyce," Michael said softly. "It'll get done."

Joanna opened the screen door. He turned with a look that oddly resembled relief.

"Where have you been?"

"Just making myself more presentable."

"Joyce, would you like something to drink?" he asked.

"A gin and tonic would be glorious."

Michael rose. "Joanna?"

"Anything."

He disappeared into the house and, uneasily, Joanna sat down in the chair beside his.

Joyce plunged into conversation right away. "While Michael's gone, I'd like to have a word with you, Joanna."

"About what?"

"As I understand it, you and your son have decided to spend the summer here."

"Yes. It was the craziest coincidence. My father wrote to—"

"Yes, I know all about that," Joyce cut in impatiently. "Michael explained the mix-up to me last Saturday night. All I want to say is, perhaps you don't realize how important it is for Michael to be here." She sat coolly, calmly, totally in command.

"Of course I do. He told me. He's writing a novel."

"A damn good novel! It could be an important piece of literature. Michael is a very talented person."

"Yes, I've always known that," Joanna said tightly, bristling at Joyce's condescension.

"Listen, I'm not asking you to leave, but please could you give him some room? Stay out of his way? Keep the house quiet? That's all I'm asking." Her eyes wandered to Casey.

"I'm doing what I can."

"Well, it's not enough. Michael's written practically nothing this week. Nothing!" Angry color climbed to Joyce's cheeks. "I can't believe he spent all yesterday afternoon fishing! And today—today I show up to find he's been romping at the beach! Joanna, *please!* I can only do so much. He's got to write the book himself, and fast. He has a deadline, you realize. It *has* to be done in three weeks."

"I hope you're not blaming me for his going fishing yesterday. It was his idea entirely."

Joyce said nothing but she was breathing heavily. Her eyes darted condemningly from Casey to Joanna as if their mere presence were cause enough for Michael to fail.

"Well, for heaven's sake, dissuade him the next time he gets a notion to go fishing. He can't waste a minute. Maybe you can even turn this living arrangement around into something positive—cook his meals, do his laundry, that sort of thing. Those of us who are close to him have to do what we can to launch his career."

Joanna could feel a vein at her temple throbbing. Was that the image she gave to strangers? Is that what she'd let herself become? Only good for cooking, washing, "that sort of thing?"

"Joyce, if you're so concerned about Michael, why don't you offer him your place? You're gone most of the week."

"I did. He was so upset last Saturday night after you showed up I didn't know what else to do. But he declined. I even offered my apartment in New York. He's always been comfortable enough there in the past . . ."

A fist closed around Joanna's heart. It was all very silly, of course. What did she care if Michael was seeing this woman? It didn't matter. She'd stopped loving him the day she left this island six years ago. Their lives had gone separate ways.

Just then, the screen door opened and Michael stepped
at into the late-afternoon sunlight. Joanna's eyes nar-
owed as if in pain as they traveled over his dark, curling
air and long muscular torso, down the corded length of his
gs and back up to his eyes. And even while she was tell-
g herself it didn't matter, her heart went soaring on an
nexpected flight and she knew she was only kidding her-
elf. It did matter—more than ever.

"Will you stay for dinner, Joyce?" Michael asked as he
t their drinks on the picnic table.

"I'd love to. I'm famished," Joyce answered, lighting a
garette.

The cogs of Joanna's mind began to whir. And who was
oing to cook that dinner? Her eyes grew mutinous. She
owned her drink with unladylike speed and shot to her
eet. "Casey, come on, sweetheart. Time to wash up."

JOANNA, WHAT GIVES?" It was half an hour later, and she
nd Casey were just leaving their bedroom, both of them
reshly showered and dressed.

She lifted her eyes with icy contempt. While she'd been
ressing, she'd heard him come up to his room—him and
is "agent!"

"Bye, Michael. Have a nice dinner."

"Hey, wait a minute." Suddenly he was angry, too. He
trode across the hall, gripped Joanna's arm, and propel-
ed her into her room.

"Casey, your mother and I have to talk. In private. Wait
ut in the hall, okay? She'll be right with you."

The boy nodded, trusting Michael unquestioningly, and
kipped toward the stair landing. Michael closed the door
nd turned, as tense as an animal about to spring.

"Listen, I can put up with your grousing when we're
lone—" he pointed a finger in her face "—but I will not
ut up with your being rude to Joyce. Grow up, for pity's
ake!"

Joanna tossed her hair over her shoulder and glared at
im. "But that's just the point. I have grown up, and I've

developed a sense of self-esteem along the way. I will ne
put up with being cast in the role of chief cook and scu
lery maid for you and . . . and that woman!''

Michael opened his mouth to protest, but she went righ
on with her well-rehearsed harangue. ''I've also develope
a set of values that will not allow me to put up with you
disgusting little bedroom games. Not under this roof! No
while Casey and I are still here!''

A muscle jumped in Michael's jaw. ''I seem to recall
time when you didn't consider my 'bedroom games' all tha
disgusting.''

Joanna's cheeks burned. ''We all learn from our mis
takes, don't we?''

''Yes, we do,'' he returned with matching conviction.

She raised her chin, hurt and proud. ''Well, it's alway
nice to find out what people really think of you.''

Michael gripped her arms, his fingers digging into th
soft flesh. ''I suppose you think you didn't have it com
ing?'' He groaned. ''Why do you make me say such things?
Dammit! Why do you still make me so angry?''

Tears sprang to her eyes before she could stop them be
cause she'd been asking herself the very same question
And at this particular moment, she didn't have the strength
to face the answer she kept coming up with. She turned her
head and fought for composure. ''This is getting us no
where. I'm simply going out to a movie with Casey to leave
you and Joyce alone.''

''No, you're not. You're angry because you assumed
you'd have to cook us dinner.''

Yes, she thought. That, and also because *their* dinner
together, hers and Michael's, had been ruined. But she
couldn't very well say that now, could she? That admission would be an act of incredible stupidity!

''I just thought you'd appreciate a little privacy, you and
Joyce. But apparently my being here doesn't seem to matter.''

His grip tightened and she winced. ''Right now, Joyce is
in my room because that's where I happen to work and

eep my manuscript. She's reading what I've done this
veek—as she does every weekend. That's all. So you can
pare me your narrow-minded lecture on ethics." His
reath fanned hotly over her face, his taut body pressing
ers. "But even if she weren't, even if she and I were about
o engage in a session of wild, abandoned lovemaking, it
vould still be none of your business. If we're going to share
his cottage like two rational adults, you've got to under-
tand that point right now."

Joanna looked hard at his face, loathing it and admir-
ng it both in the same confused moment. "Over my dead
ody!"

His mouth twitched, suppressing a smile. "That can be
rranged, you know."

"Oh, you'd love that, wouldn't you? If I weren't here,
hen you and your . . . your little tootsie would have the run
of the place." His amusement deepened. "But tell me, Michael, does she realize you're just using her to further your
career? How long will it be before you dump her?"

Now he laughed openly. "Is that a serious accusation, or
are you just fishing to find out how involved we are?"

"I couldn't care less how involved you are." Joanna was
trembling and knew he could feel it; he was standing so
close. "You can sleep with every woman from here to
Mexico for all I care. But not in this house!"

Michael's hand moved to the back of her head and dug
into the heavy thickness of her hair. She was sure he was
going to yank. But instead, he sighed and dropped his
forehead to hers.

"Joanna, Joanna! Why do you still have the power to
burrow so deep under my skin? After all this time . . ."

She tilted her head back in amazement, her lips parting
as she did. On a wave of white heat, she realized what they
were doing. He was holding her in his arms and their lips
were just inches apart.

His eyes became intense and smoldering as if the real-
ization had just struck him, too. A moment later, he had
lowered his head and his mouth was touching hers. She

gave a cry, but it was only halfhearted. She felt his arm enclose her more tightly, imprisoning her against the warm hard length of his body, and his kiss deepened. Her body went weak under his bruising hunger; her bones turned to water. Michael's kiss affected her the way nothing else ever had. It was as if all the years that had separated them had never existed, and she responded with an ardor that was humiliating.

Slowly Michael lifted his head. They were both breathing erratically, their eyes glazed with desire. Joanna felt dizzy and rested her head on his chest. His fingers trailed along her spine.

"Jo, I'm not sure I know what's happening here," he whispered unsteadily. "I'm not sure I want to find out, either."

She swallowed with difficulty and drew back. She couldn't look at him. "Then you'd better go. Joyce will be wondering what's become of you."

He nodded and opened the door.

CHAPTER TEN

IT WASN'T LATE when she and Casey returned home, yet Joyce had already left and Michael had gone to bed. The sleep clearly did him good because Joanna awoke the next morning to the sound of his typewriter. Quietly she got Casey breakfast, then they left to pick up Meg and her children for a day at the beach.

When she got back in the middle of the afternoon, she was relieved to hear Michael still up in his room. Her reaction to him the previous evening was still disturbing her tremendously. How could she have let herself lose control like that? After the humiliating, hurtful way he'd treated her, after all the years of simmering resentment that had followed, was it possible she could still feel physically attracted to him?

Obviously he wasn't immune to her, either. The kiss had been unpremeditated, unexpected, and she could still feel the heat of it.

But really, did it mean anything? Michael was a physical person. He always had been; he probably couldn't hold *any* woman without reacting that way. She'd simply been the woman he happened to be holding at the moment. And as far as she was concerned, well, perhaps she'd just been living without a man's touch for too long.

They had made a mistake last night, and not an easy one to forget, but now she was forewarned. She was sure that with a little vigilance, it would never happen again.

She was staring into the refrigerator wondering what to fix for dinner when she heard Casey's excited chatter up in

Michael's room. With a groan, she left the kitchen an
went to fetch him.

"Sorry about this, Michael," she said as Casey shuffle
slowly out to the hall.

"No problem." He went on typing.

"Aren't you going to take a break?" she asked, pausin
in the doorway.

"Can't afford to. Joyce read me the riot act last night."

"She's a tough lady."

He pushed away from his desk, revealing the clutter be
fore him—a mountain of crumpled paper, a coffee mug anc
two TV dinner trays.

"I know," he said. "But she's good for me."

She'd been right. The kiss really hadn't meant anythin
to him. Without another word, she made her exit.

Downstairs, Joanna checked the refrigerator one mor
time before finally grabbing her car keys and heading fo
the nearest seafood market. She knew buying lobster wa
an extravagance, but she was sick to death of scrimping
Besides, indulging oneself occasionally was good for the
ego—therapeutic even. And when it came to benevolen
indulgence, she was certainly overdue.

As she returned to the cottage, however, she couldn't
help recalling Joyce's suggestion that she do Michael's
cooking. Sitting on the back seat, clawing menacingly
against the thick paper bag, were three large lobsters.
Three, not two.

But Joanna dismissed Joyce's words immediately. Be
fore she'd even met Joyce, she'd already come to the con
clusion that cooking separate meals was a waste of time and
energy. Besides, she was *not* doing this for Michael. She
was doing it for herself.

When Michael finally came down the stairs, rubbing his
aching neck, the table was all set—the baked potatoes, the
crisp salad and warm garlic bread, chilled white wine, hot
melted butter, and the platter of steaming red lobsters.

He paused in midstep. "A-are you having company?"

"No. Come and eat before it gets cold," she answered brusquely, not wanting him to read anything into her efforts.

He approached the table hesitantly, as if he still didn't believe her. Then, "What a wonderful surprise!" He smiled softly and the strain and fatigue eased from his handsome face.

Joanna was sure it was the most delicious meal she had ever cooked. She cleaned her plate, every last succulent, buttery mouthful. Michael evidently felt the same. He even finished off what Casey left. She was glad. And, though the admission came slowly, she finally realized that it *pleased* her to make him happy—Joyce be hanged; it was not just some altruistic concern for his health or burgeoning career. It pleased her, deeply.

Finally they sat back, replete, smiling at each other over a heap of empty red shells. Peace pervaded the room.

"Thank you for a lovely dinner," Michael said, leaning over to touch his napkin to the corner of her mouth. She was embarrassed to find herself leaning into his touch, longing for it to stay. All through the meal, she had felt a growing awareness of him, until at times she'd been unable to concentrate. At times she'd found herself listening not so much to his words but rather to the rise and fall of his deep voice. She had been caught up in the myriad expressions of his face, utterly fascinated by and lost in his personality.

"A far cry from our dinner last Saturday." She shuddered at the memory of his oily chicken soup and her muddy stew.

His mouth lifted in an endearing, crooked smile. "What a difference a week makes!"

"Yes, well..." She looked away uneasily. Had it only been one week? How much had changed! How much she had discovered locked up within herself—and him!

"I'd better get moving. I'm supposed to be going to a concert with Nathan tonight."

Michael's long, dark lashes lowered over suddenly troubled eyes.

"Sandy is coming to stay with Casey again."

He nodded, his finger tracing an invisible pattern in the tablecloth. "Go on. Go get ready. I'll clean up."

"Thanks." She rose quickly, afraid if she lingered even a moment longer, she wouldn't go at all.

NATHAN KISSED JOANNA at the door that night. She had sensed he would all evening and didn't discourage him. She was curious to see what her reaction would be.

She shouldn't have wondered. Though she was sure Nathan was quite adept at what he was doing, his advances left her cold. As he drove away, dismay settled heavily on her heart.

Much to her relief, the next few days passed uneventfully. She couldn't forget the kiss she and Michael had exchanged. And she couldn't imagine Michael forgetting it, either. Just thinking about it sometimes rocked her to the foundation of her equilibrium. However, the more unsettling her emotions, the harder she worked at hiding them. Evidently Michael had also decided to ignore their encounter. If he thought about it—and from the way he occasionally looked at her, she was sure he did—he never said anything. After a few days, she felt immeasurably better.

Michael worked on his book from morning to night now, and Joanna usually took Casey out to the beach all day. In the evening, she cooked a healthful meal for them all, fearing that if she didn't, Michael would forget to eat altogether. These days, he was working as if driven.

One morning she found him out on the sun porch. His face was drawn and serious.

"Taking a break?"

He looked up slowly. Dark shadows deepened his eyes. "Jo, I don't know if I'm going to finish it."

Joanna knew Joyce had been calling regularly, but her pep talks only left him keyed-up and pacing the floor.

She lowered herself onto the cushioned settee beside him. "And if you don't?"

"Gateway will have every legal right to cancel my contract."

"Will you get serious! They wouldn't do anything as drastic as that."

"Maybe not, but Joyce's credibility will be damaged. She really went out on a limb for me."

"I wish you were as concerned about your own career as you are about hers."

Michael fell back tiredly against the nautical print cushions. "I am, I am. That's just it. I've just been wondering if I'm going to finish it at all. It's just not . . . coming." He closed his eyes, his last few words sounding so desperate.

Joanna looked at him, and though she'd been running from her feelings for days, her heart now filled with a yearning to reach out to him. For once, she stopped fighting herself and admitted she wanted to take him in her arms and hold him close.

But she didn't dare. All she said was, "I think you're working too hard."

"Oh?"

"You're forcing it. You've got to relax, get some physical exercise."

He cocked open one eye. "And what would you suggest?"

"Well . . . jogging, swimming, rowing. I put my dad's old rowboat in the water this week, you know."

"Aw, hell!" He snapped his fingers. "And here I was thinking you had something more interesting in mind."

She swatted his leg in mock exasperation, though inwardly she was glad to see his spirits lifting. He caught her hand and drew the palm to his lips. Their eyes met and Joanna felt a surge of excitement that made her head spin.

"Maybe you're right. Joyce's way obviously isn't working."

Self-consciously, she drew back her hand, aware that the brief touch had left her tingling all over. "Michael?"

"Hmm?"

"Why don't you bring your work down to the dining-room table? There's more room. Besides, I'll be able to watch Casey better from there while I'm helping you."

His eyes widened. "What did you say?"

"I'm no speed demon, but I type a heck of a lot faster than you do."

His expression brightened, and a smile lit his blue eyes. "Yeah?"

"Yeah."

"Be right down." He took the stairs two at a time.

They immersed themselves in their collaboration that very afternoon. Though plot-wise Joanna couldn't make much sense out of what she typed that day, since she was starting with chapter seventeen, Michael's writing still stunned her. After dinner that evening she sat on the sun porch and began reading at the beginning.

Joyce was right, she thought. Michael really was a gifted writer, and this, this was an extraordinary novel—funny and lyrical and driving. About halfway through, a lump tightened in Joanna's throat and nothing she could do would make it go away.

It was an introspective story, a contemporary drama of a young divorced man trying to cope with his disheveled life. Michael? she wondered. The main character was, after all, a teacher.

Michael joined her on the porch just as she was starting the chapter she'd typed that day. Tears were trickling silently down her cheeks.

"That bad, huh?"

At that moment Joanna didn't think she had ever felt so melancholy, or so inspired, or so proud in her entire life. She tried to say something but her lips trembled too badly and the tears kept pouring from her eyes. All she could do was raise her hand toward him.

He walked over and let her wrap her arms around his waist. He leaned down and kissed the top of her head. Slowly he lifted her from the chair and folded her close to him, rocking her back and forth. It was almost as if he were consoling her, she thought.

Did he know how defeated she felt just then, how dazzled by his style and sensitive insights? Did he realize how aware she was of his strength of character? He must. Reading his novel had been a startlingly intimate experience, like living inside his skin, thinking with his mind. And she had been alive for every second of it, alive in a way she had never been before. And the fact that she could no longer hide her feelings behind a facade of pride or independence—or anger—made her feel so very, well, *defeated*!

Michael eased away from her a little and smoothed back her hair. His hands were warm and secure, cradling her head. He was smiling, and his eyes were glittering over her face as if he had, indeed, finally conquered something. Then he kissed each eyelid softly, drew her closer, and kissed her lips. Joanna felt a weightless, bottoming-out sensation in her stomach, a dizziness in her head. And then the warmth began, that wonderful, debilitating heat that made her press closer...

Only to be cut off when Michael pulled back abruptly. He took a deep, fortifying breath and looked away from her. "You'd better get some sleep. I'd like us to get an early start tomorrow."

Joanna was startled to feel disappointment crashing down around her. Yet she managed a small smile and a nod before heading for her room.

The days soon fell into a routine. All morning long, sometimes till two or three in the afternoon, Michael would write and pace the porch, then write some more, and Joanna, at the dining-room table, would type. Then they would break for the rest of the afternoon and take Casey swimming or rowing or hiking. Sometimes they simply took long rides in Michael's car. Then in the evening, after a meal they usually prepared together, Joanna would do the dishes and laundry while he sat in his favorite corner of the sun porch rereading and revising what they had done ear-

lier that day. Joanna had never realized what a tedious
back-and-forth movement this business of writing was.

Oddly enough, he seemed to be making more progress
now than he had when he'd been working longer hours.
Not only that, his skin was turning the smooth, deep gold
she remembered envying so much when she was a girl. His
appetite was ravenous, too, from all the exercise he was
getting in the salt sea air.

Casey behaved extremely well while they were working,
especially as they were able to give him very little attention
these days. Most of the time he played contentedly in the
yard where they could see him, building imaginary roads
and bridges in the sandy soil for his cars and trucks to
travel. And one afternoon, Michael came home from a
mysterious shopping trip with a small inflatable pool.

Joanna couldn't help laughing at the purchase, considering how close they were to the beach. But since Casey
couldn't venture off alone, it only made sense. At times, in
fact, he seemed to enjoy the pool much more than the
beach. It was an ocean just the right size to launch his fleet
of toy boats.

He was doing so well these days, she thought. There
wasn't a single reference to Phil that didn't indicate a com-
plete acceptance of his death, not one unreasonable tear
since the incident with the seashell. Perhaps the island was
working its healing magic after all.

On her, too, she realized. She was unquestionably happy,
happier than she'd been in—yes, if she was really honest—
years.

Nathan called nearly every evening, but Joanna made
polite excuses when he asked her out. She could have found
the time, she supposed, but she was afraid he was jumping
to conclusions about their relationship. Probably, she
thought with a pang of guilt, because of the kiss that had
ended their last date. She didn't claim to understand her
reaction. Nathan Trent was considered quite a catch. He
was personable, good-looking, had his own thriving busi-

ness, a beautiful home, and he was family-oriented. Yet, he just didn't . . . fit! They were gears that didn't quite mesh.

Only once in her life had she felt that way—only once. That deep abiding harmony . . .

There were moments when she paused in her typing and wondered if Michael ever thought about that time in their lives, too. He looked as if he did. At times, a disconcerting warmth entered his eyes. As he passed her chair, she sometimes felt the touch of his hand. . . .

And then she'd think of those unguarded moments of affection they'd recently shared. And her heart would start wondering what it all meant.

But these were dangerous thoughts, insidious thoughts. Michael was seeing Joyce Sterling these days, a woman who seemed to take nothing casually, least of all a personal relationship.

But even if his relationship with Joyce was just a casual affair, was she wise in letting herself speculate about Michael and herself? She knew what he was like from bitter experience. The past could not be changed. And the truth was that Michael could not be trusted or believed.

The only trouble was . . . she was afraid she was in love with him again. No, not *again*. Her love had probably never ended. Like all the other emotional baggage she'd been carrying around since she'd run away from here, her love had probably always been with her, way down there under the surface of her life. Otherwise, why had she still been so hurt over Michael's deceit? Why had she still been so angry? Those feelings didn't make sense anymore. No, it was precisely *because* she still loved him that she'd felt so devastated and enraged.

One thing was clear, though. She had to keep this insight to herself. If Michael found out she still loved him, she wasn't sure exactly what he'd do. But he'd used her once before, and as far as she was concerned, once was enough for an entire lifetime.

CHAPTER ELEVEN

IT WAS THE MIDDLE of the following week, five days before his deadline, when Michael finished the novel. He was leaning over Joanna, reading the last few sentences as she typed them, and he made the announcement.

"That's it. I'm not going to fuss anymore. That's it."

She half turned and looked up at him. "What?"

"I'm through with revisions. Just type 'The End' and let's be done with it."

She did as she was told and sat back. Michael had strolled to the sun-porch door and was staring out toward the pond.

It had been quite an experience for Joanna, tiring and tedious but oddly exhilarating. Even though she looked forward to spending more time with Casey now, she was still sorry her job was done. She could only imagine what Michael was feeling.

"What happens now?" she asked, lifting her long hair off her neck. The weather had turned hot and oppressively humid. Her T-shirt and shorts clung to her uncomfortably.

"I'll give Joyce a call and let her know," he said distractedly.

But of course. Always Joyce. She should be used to it by now.

"She'll be here in a couple of days. I'll drop the manuscript off with her, and she can take it back to New York on Sunday."

Joanna's tired shoulders slumped with a sense of anticlimax. Michael had just finished his novel, yet he was acting as if it were just an ordinary day. She had expected a little more excitement, a few unrestrained whoops of joy, maybe even a "Gee-I couldn't-have-done-it-without-you-kid." But—nothing?

Michael scooped up the phone, sat on the stairs and dialed.

"Joyce Sterling, please."

Joanna picked up a few crumpled papers from the floor and stuffed them into an already full wastebasket.

"Hi, Joyce? Michael." He was smiling.

She moved the typewriter to the floor, the manuscript to the sideboard, and then polished away the coffee rings and eraser crumbs accumulated over the past two dreamlike weeks.

"Yes, that's why I'm calling," Michael's deep voice rumbled on, warm and sexy.

Joanna sprayed and polished again. The room was beginning to look as if nothing had happened there.

"I'll leave it with you Saturday. You are coming to the Vineyard this weekend, aren't you?"

Joanna glanced up from the polished table. He had a look on his face that was all too familiar. She really should take a picture of it and hang it on her wall as a constant reminder. She could caption it "Michael Malone on the Make."

"A party? You don't have to do that..."

She put away the dust cloth and told herself she didn't really want to cry. So what if Michael didn't want to celebrate with her? Joyce deserved to share that special moment much more than she did. Joyce was his agent. She had gone to bat for him on a partial manuscript. She had negotiated a terrific contract.

"Excuse me." She tried to pass Michael on the stairs, but he looked up and motioned for her to wait.

Then covering the receiver, he told her Joyce wanted to talk to her. "She's having a celebration party this weekend, and she'd like you to go."

"Me?" she mouthed silently.

"Yes. Here. She wants to talk to you."

Joanna sat on the step above Michael's and took the receiver. Of course Joyce wanted Joanna to go. And bring along a friend. It would be just an informal gathering of friends and business associates.

Joyce was actually very gracious. But then, she had no reason not to be. She was undoubtedly quite confident in her relationship with Michael. If she suspected anything about Joanna's past, she certainly didn't fear it.

As soon as she got off the phone with Joyce, Joanna called Nathan. She was glad Michael had wandered out to the kitchen. Unfortunately he returned too soon.

"You can make it?" she was saying. "Oh, great! I really didn't want to go to something like that alone. Thanks a million."

Oddly, Michael's smile vanished. "You asked Nathan Trent to Joyce's party?" he asked when she was off the phone.

"Y-yes. Joyce said I should bring a date."

"So?"

"So, who did you expect me to ask?"

He gave her a look she couldn't explain, and yet it shook her to her very soul. Only as he was turning and heading back into the kitchen did she notice the bottle of champagne and the two glasses in his hand.

JOANNA RODE to Joyce's cottage the following Saturday evening in a quietly distracted state, but Nathan hardly noticed. He parked in the circular driveway and got out to open her door. Quickly she glanced in the mirror. She had taken such care with her makeup and clothing, but still she felt insecure.

She was wearing a new, ice-blue silk dress with a softly gathered skirt and halter top. It had been last year's stock at her store and she'd bought it at a fraction of the original cost. It was the most alluring dress she owned, but she'd never worn it before, and Michael had left too early for her to get a critique. Of course, Nathan's eyes had registered

tal delight. But then they always did, whether she was
earing an alluring dress or simply a pair of old jeans.

The front door was open and people were gathered in
mall groups around the living room, talking and laughing
ghtly as ice cubes clinked in their glasses. One of them was
Michael, looking tall and attractive and utterly masculine.
1 fact, he dominated the room with his air of authority
nd his stunning good looks. She was surprised by this facet
f him. He looked so . . . so urbane! And it occurred to her
1at she'd never seen him dressed this way before, in dress
ants, shirt and tie.

As soon as he saw them, he walked over, his eyes sweep-
1g her like a searchlight, swift and brilliant. "You're
ooking very nice tonight," he said with a polite smile. "I
on't think I've ever seen that dress before." He quickly
urned to Nathan, cutting Joanna off before she could say
nything in reply. "Joyce is out back with the rest of the
uests. Let me introduce you around."

He led them through the tastefully modern living room
o glass sliders that opened onto a flagstoned patio. A
lozen people were mingling there, but Joanna saw only
oyce. Tonight her rich brown hair was coiled at her nape
nd she wore a silk caftan in butterfly colors, which, on
anyone else, might appear gaudy but on her became a
masterpiece of design. Her bearing was regal. She talked
with an ease that Joanna envied.

Their eyes met and Joyce's smile froze. She cocked her
head and glanced speculatively over Joanna and the two
men by her side.

"Joyce, I'd like you to meet Joanna's friend Nathan
Trent," Michael introduced smoothly, every inch the so-
cial counterpart of his hostess.

Nathan shook the woman's hand and smiled. "It was
very nice of you to invite us."

"Very nice of you to come." Still smiling, she flicked
another cool glance over Joanna. "I hear you're the owner
of those charming little boutiques that carry all those wonderful English wools."

Nathan was flattered and talked for several minutes about his shops. But eventually another couple arrived and Joyce's keen eyes captured Michael's. He nodded, communicating on a level that needed no words. Joanna's chest tightened.

"Excuse us, please," Joyce said, taking Michael's arm. "I have to introduce Michael to someone, but do make yourselves comfortable. Help yourselves at the bar." She drifted off, with Michael at her side.

At first, Joanna found mingling difficult. While Joyce's gathering wasn't large, it certainly was illustrious. Several writers and artists who lived on the island were there, as were politicians, magazine people, and business associates from New York. But once they discovered who Joanna was, or rather who her housemate was, they opened up to her in a way she found almost amusing.

It didn't take long to realize this was no ordinary celebration among friends. Joyce had deliberately gathered these people together as a public-relations move. She wanted these influential people in the arts and media to get to know her dashing young client. Joyce had orchestrated the whole thing for his benefit. She had even invited Douglas McCrory, the publisher of Gateway Books.

Joanna was sorry she'd come. Joyce was not only beautiful and intelligent, but she was also a vital force in Michael's career. They made a perfect couple, blending in a way she and Michael never could.

Joanna drank liberally, but it did little to dull her senses. No matter where she was or who she talked to, she remained aware of Michael's presence in the crowd. Aware, too, of his disapproving frown whenever their eyes met. She tried to talk to him once, but after a few desultory remarks, he excused himself and walked away. Was he ashamed of her? Did he not want to be associated with her in front of these people?

Well, she would be damned if she'd allow him to intimidate her. Even if she wasn't part of this crowd, she had nothing to be ashamed of. She had always been considered irly intelligent and creative herself. And she certainly adn't been locked in a vacuum the past six years. She had ad nearly a book a week and she'd been on a committee the library that organized lectures and slide shows. Even orking at the store had had its advantages; she had met nd talked with people from every walk of life, from the rthest corners of the globe.

By ten-thirty, however, she'd had it! "Nathan, do you ink we can leave now?"

"Sure, honey. Let's go say our goodbyes."

They found Joyce on the fringe of the gathering talking ith Mr. McCrory. Michael was by her side—as he had een nearly all evening.

Joanna lifted her chin and dredged up yet one more mile. "Joyce, we're going to be leaving now." She avoided Michael's cool gaze.

"What, so soon?"

Nathan grinned and his hand drifted to Joanna's waist. 'Well, I haven't seen this little lady in nearly two weeks. ou know how it is."

Joyce laughed, giving Michael a quick glance. "I cerainly do. Oh, before you go, I'd like to thank you, Joanna."

"Me? For what?"

"For helping Michael. I hear you've been quite the busy ypist."

Joanna looked at Michael. Yes, she had certainly yped—but she'd done more than that. She had encouraged him, cajoled, even made some fairly candid remarks that had inspired a few important pages.

And then there were all those wonderful, golden afternoons rowing on the pond, and the giggles that accompanied cooking dinner, and later the quiet, peaceful talks on the porch... Somehow she sensed they had helped even more than the typing had.

But Michael's eyes returned none of this. No defense, no gratitude. She might have been a stranger to him.

Fighting back a new wave of rejection, she smiled va
iantly. "Well, it's nothing compared to what you're doin
for him."

Joyce smiled like the proverbial cat with the cream.

"Good night," Nathan said. "Again, thanks for havir
us."

Joanna turned and walked away, feeling the bitter stin
of tears in her throat.

LATER THAT NIGHT, after Nathan had gone, Joanna war
dered out to the front porch. Casey was sleeping over a
Meg's tonight, and she had the whole place to herself. Un
doubtedly she wouldn't be seeing Michael for a while to
night—if at all!

A gigantic moon was glowing in the sky, its light spar
kling across the crushed seashells in the driveway. She sa
down on the top step and carefully folded her silky skir
around her ankles. There was an unearthly luminescence on
everything, all the low brambles from here to the sea. Ever
insect sounds seemed silvered with the light.

She leaned her head against the rail and sighed, thinkin
back to Joyce's party. She was still hurt by the way Mi
chael had ignored her. Hadn't she fit in with this crowd? O
was Joyce so fascinating that he hadn't even been aware o
the way he'd snubbed her? Maybe she just didn't exist fo
him outside this cottage. Maybe that's how it had always
been—a limited, summer-cottage relationship.

Joanna blinked at the stinging in her eyes. She loved
Michael so much at this moment, and the truth was she
wanted him to love her in return. She wanted to be a part
of his life. She didn't want to go back to New Hampshire.
She wanted to stay here with him—forever. And it hurt so
much knowing that she couldn't, knowing he didn't want
her.

Joanna listened to the low thunder of the waves, feeling
more and more bereft. Their hypnotic rhythm carried her

er the dunes and away, back to a night six years ago when ichael had not been so immune...

It had been a night much like this one, a night so still and ltry the air felt like velvet on their skin. They'd gone wn to the beach after dinner and were lying together ithin the folds of a thick blanket, staring hypnotized into ch other's eyes...

"Joanna?" she remembered him whispering.

"Yes?"

"Nothing. I just wanted to say your name. I love the und of it."

And she had laughed and told him it was an awful name, plain and old-fashioned.

But he'd shaken his head. "To me it's the loveliest word naginable. Joanna. Three little syllables that can turn me ompletely inside out..."

A tear trickled down Joanna's cheek as she remembered at night, how his eyes had seared into hers with such rugging intensity, how their arms had wrapped so tightly round each other, their damp legs entwined. Even now, he could feel his hard masculine strength over every inch f her body....

"Jo, do you realize how deeply in love I am with you?" e had whispered. "It's different from anything else I've ver felt. We're so close I feel...I feel married to you."

"I love you, too, Michael. I'll always love you."

"Forever," he'd vowed. "We *are* married, Jo, in a way hat's far more binding than a civil license. I really believe t. In a spiritual, mystical way, you and I are husband and vife."

"Oh, Michael! If only it were true!"

He'd smiled softly and then got to his feet.

"What are you doing?" she'd asked.

"Here, this will have to do." In his hand was a clump of eaweed.

"What?"

"Your flowers, ma'am." He'd bowed elegantly. "W~~ you said you wanted to get married..."

When she'd continued to stare at him, he'd pulled her and thrust the brittle bouquet into her hand. Then h~~ draped the sandy blanket over her shoulders "for a gown

"Michael, sometimes I swear you're crazy!"

But he was undaunted. He even waxed poetic, exagge ating his gestures comically. "The ocean's murmur will our music, my love, this sacred beach our church."

"And the minister?" she'd asked.

Joanna still remembered the serious look that had ov~~ taken his expression, eyes wandering over the moo glittering sea and up to the stars. "He's here. He's liste ing."

He'd taken her hand then and held it in both of his, clo~~ to his heart. "Joanna, I don't know exactly how the wor~~ go, but I think it all comes down to this—I love you. You'~~ my soul, my body's breath, my life's joy. And I guess I' yours from this day forward, completely and forever."

Joanna had stared into his eyes, eyes so deep and since~~ and loving she almost couldn't speak. "And I'm your Michael, completely and forever. Wherever we go, wha ever we do, apart or together, throughout time into ete nity, we'll be as one."

On that hot, languid night six years ago, Michael te~~ derly and sensitively carried her over the threshold of fu~~ womanhood on a wave of emotional and physical ecstas she had never dreamed possible. Their lovemaking left he limp in his arms and sobbing quietly, but she was happie~~ she was sure, than anyone else who had ever walked th earth before her. She was irrevocably his, branded by him indelibly molded by his body and his love.

Now as Joanna gazed out over the moon-washed land scape, tears streamed silently down her hot cheeks. Why di~~ she have to remember that silly ceremony now? Such flow ery, formal vows! Such hopelessly idealistic nonsense! I

d meant nothing! Michael had mocked those vows within
eeks—indeed, had been mocking them all along.

Then, why did she remember the details of that night so
vidly? And why, after all that had intervened, did she feel
ven now this vital, unbreakable bond?

Joanna was startled out of her thoughts by the beam of
headlight bouncing up the driveway. She wiped her wet
heeks quickly, recognizing the sound of the engine.

Michael's Volvo came to a skidding stop and he vaulted
ut, slamming the door angrily. He took two long strides
efore he noticed her curled up on the stairs.

"Oh. You're alone?"

"Yes." She was alarmed at the sudden sense of excite-
ent shooting through her nerves.

Slowly he loosened his tie and undid the top button of his
hirt. "Good. We're going to have to talk."

CHAPTER TWELVE

MICHAEL LOWERED HIMSELF to the step beside her. All
Joanna's senses were alive and ringing with an awareness ⟨
him.

"What do you want to talk about?"

"You and Nathan."

"Michael, did you come rushing home just to give n
another lecture on how a respectable widow should b
have?"

"Yes...no! Of course not! Listen, I know I get pret
upset when you butt into my affairs—or at least I used to—
and I have no right butting into yours, but...dammit, J⟨
anna!" He thrust a hand through his hair, raking it bac
from his forehead. "I just want to warn you to watch ou
for yourself. You're going through a transitional period i
your life and you're vulnerable. I'd hate to see you g⟨
hurt."

Considering her emotional state, Joanna turned a r⟨
markably calm stare on him. "Oh? And what makes yo
so sure I'm going to get hurt?"

Michael shrugged. "I'm not. I can't tell how seriou
you're getting or what Nathan's intentions are." And whe
she didn't answer, "Well?"

"You were right. It's none of your business."

"Dammit, Jo! Will you level with me!"

"Why? You didn't level with me when I asked abou
Joyce."

He subsided with a guilty look. "You're right, and
should have. I detect a little misunderstanding where Joyc⟨
is concerned."

"I doubt it."

"Well, you're wrong. There's nothing between me and Joyce, nothing except a business relationship. We're not lovers and never have been. I won't deny that we've gone out together socially a few times, and maybe she was hoping it would turn into something more. But it never did. And I've never led her to think otherwise."

Relief and joy swept through Joanna even while she was trying to remind herself to be careful. "Then why the big fascination with her tonight?"

Michael's brow furrowed. "What do you mean?"

"You know what I mean. You never left her side for a minute. And me...? You treated me as if I had leprosy." She tossed her hair over her shoulder, feeling it swing heavily against her back.

Michael leaned his elbows on his knees and stared broodingly down the road. "You didn't suffer by it. You managed to make your presence felt."

She glared at his moon-washed profile. "I refuse to let you bully me into thinking I did anything wrong. I looked as presentable as anybody else. I didn't say anything dumb or uncouth—"

"Will you shut up for once and listen? That's the trouble with you! You go on and on about how *you* see things, and you never listen to what anyone else is saying."

Joanna laughed mirthlessly. "And why should I? Whenever I listen to you, I hear insulting things, like I'm a lonely ol' widow who's letting men take advantage and—"

Michael didn't give her a chance to finish. He grabbed her arms, pulled her to him and silenced her with a kiss. Joanna gave a muffled cry and went stiff with instinctive resistance.

When he finally let her go, she gasped, "Michael, you're out of your mind!" So he kissed her again. This time, however, she knew her willpower was abandoning her.

She could feel the firm pliancy of his lips as they moved over hers, could feel what his warmth was doing to her body. Her heart was beating against his chest like a ham-

mer, and her blood was turning to fire. When he at
tempted to draw away, it was she who clung and held him
close.

"You don't play fair," she moaned as his lips brushed
hers with tantalizing softness.

"I learned the rules from you, love." His lips left hers to
trail along her cheek to her ear. "Why did you have to look
so beautiful tonight, hmm? If I hadn't stayed away from
you, I'm afraid I would have done this right on Joyce's patio. This, or broken a few bones in Nathan's body."

Again he kissed her, long and deep, and Joanna didn't
try to protest. She loved the feelings he was arousing in her.

"Michael?" she whispered. "Just for the record, there's
nothing between me and Nathan, either. Not on my part
anyway. I asked him to Joyce's party simply because I
didn't know who else to ask, and I didn't want to go without an escort."

Michael shook his head and laughed. "You're hopeless!
I just assumed we . . . I mean, after the way we've been getting along lately . . ."

"That we'd be going together?"

"Of course. That's another reason I was so ticked off
tonight."

So, it hadn't been just her imagination! Something really
had been happening between them these past two weeks
while they'd been working on the novel. Wasn't life
strange? she thought vaguely as he pulled her close again.
Wasn't it awfully, wonderfully strange!

This time when he kissed her, his tongue began a hot ex-
ploration of her mouth. She cried out softly and dug her
fingers into his hair, drawing him even closer. She was dizzy
with the masculine fragrance of his skin, mindless with the
ecstasy of knowing he wanted her—and had, even at
Joyce's party.

He tipped her back onto the floor of the porch and lay
alongside her. His hand caressed her with gentle intimacy,
yet there was an underlying urgency in his touch that was
exciting, igniting a fever wherever it went.

When he undid the strap of her halter, however, her old doubts surged to the surface one more time. Hadn't she learned anything from the past? Hadn't all her troubles started just this way?

"Michael, don't." She sat up, fumbling with the loosened ties.

But he sat up behind her and kissed the side of her face, lifting her hair to brush his lips over her neck. She closed her eyes, dropped her hands and surrendered to the delicious heat washing through her. Michael must have felt the slackening of her body, because his lips moved more persistently to her ear, exploring its sensitive curves with a sensual slowness that soon had her weak and breathless again.

"Michael, stop. This is madness," she said, her voice hoarse with longing.

He turned her around in his arms. "This isn't madness, Jo," he said against her soft, responsive mouth. "This is the sanest, most honest thing that's ever happened between us, and it's too beautiful to keep fighting."

Joanna didn't want to fight it, either. Holding him, kissing him—that was what she longed for with every fiber of her being.

"Jo, I don't want to want you as much as I do," he whispered raggedly. "I wish I could get you out of my system. You've never been anything but trouble to me. But you're like a fever in my blood. You're driving me crazy...." His last words were muffled against her mouth, and when Joanna began to kiss him again, he shuddered through his entire body.

"You've grown so beautiful...it's been pure torture being with you and not being able to hold you this way. If only you knew how many times I've wanted to do this—to stop whatever we were doing and pull you into my arms..." Again he kissed her, and again the effect was like a minor earthquake through her nervous system.

"Jo, I'd come to think I'd never hold you like this again," he said huskily. "I'd never feel your wonderful

body or see your beautiful face..." He pulled her closer
the heat of his body seeking the heat in hers. "You make
me feel so alive again...as if all these years I've been
dead..." He slid down the soft material of her dress and the
moonlight bathed her breasts.

Somewhere at the back of her mind, a small voice was
trying to say she was being reckless, that this could lead to
nothing but pain. She had to make him stop, had to make
herself stop. But the voice was so faint and what it was
saying seemed irrelevant now. Michael wanted her; something was still there between them, something beautiful and
strong and enduring. Maybe in the few weeks they had left,
they could build on that. Maybe this time things would
work out for them after all. She couldn't think of past hurts
anymore. There were too many other feelings crowding out
the pain—love and joy, and most wonderful of all, hope.

Her mind swimming through a haze of passion, she was
vaguely aware of being carried into the house and up the
stairs to his room. Moonlight, slanting in through the window, washed over the bed. Michael laid her down and for
a moment just stood there gazing at her. So much was in his
eyes, Joanna thought—desire, sincerity, admiration—no,
it was nearly an adoration.

"Are you sure you want to do this, Jo?" he asked softly.

She smiled and raised her hand to him. How she loved
this man! And she would go on loving him till the end of
her days. There was nothing she could do to stop it. This
was *right*; it was an acknowledgement of their future, not
just their past.

He sat on the edge of the bed beside her. Slowly Joanna
removed his tie and tossed it on the floor. Then she unbut-
toned his shirt and ran her fingers through the crisp, dark
hair of his chest. Michael closed his eyes and moaned
softly.

He took her hands and kissed their palms. Then he
leaned down and captured her mouth with a savage sweet-

ness that scattered the very last fragments of her doubts or inhibitions. With a gentle tug, her dress slipped silkily over her legs and off the bed. A moment later his trousers followed.

"I want you so much, Jo." His voice was breathlessly urgent now. Lying close beside him, she could feel his body trembling with tightly controlled passion. "It's been so long since I've been able to do anything except conjure you up in my mind. I can hardly believe you're here...." He took a deep, shuddering breath. "Oh, my beautiful Joanna..."

Emotion reached too high a pitch for any further words. Soon they were soaring to new heights of sensation, and when sensation finally peaked in ecstasy, Joanna felt certain she and Michael had melded inextricably, body, mind, and soul into one person.

JOANNA WOKE LATE the next morning. She had slept soundly, wrapped in an inexplicable feeling of well-being. When she opened her eyes and saw Michael asleep beside her, she smiled and remembered why. She leaned up on one elbow and stared down at his devilishly handsome face. Even in sleep he managed to look sexy, she thought with a laugh.

His absurdly long eyelashes fluttered. "Oh, hi there." He smiled sleepily, rolling toward her and nuzzling her hair. "What time is it?"

"After ten."

They lay for a peaceful moment, without speaking. Joanna couldn't help feeling secure this bright morning, cherished and...complete! She wondered if she should be disgusted with herself for succumbing to him so easily, if she should be sick with worrying where this step was taking her. But she wasn't. She couldn't be. Michael had been right: their lovemaking really was the most honest part of their long and muddled relationship. It was natural and beautiful, and Joanna no longer wanted to drown out what it was trying to tell her.

"When's Casey due home?" Michael's eyes were gleaming, a small, teasing smile on his lips.

"Not till around noon." She began to smile, too, exquisitely aware of the hard length of his body alongside hers. He leaned over her, his tanned, muscular shoulders made golden by the morning sunlight. He kissed her long and deeply, then raised his head in order to look at her again. Joanna couldn't tell which was more arousing—that incredible, debilitating kiss of his, or the look in his eyes.

She wrapped him in a tight embrace, loving him so much that tears sprang to her eyes.

Suddenly the sound of the phone shattered the cool morning stillness. Michael groaned and his head fell heavily on her bare shoulder. It rang again. They looked at each other questioningly.

"Forget it," Michael said. "Let it ring."

"But it might be important."

"So is this." Michael lowered his head and kissed her into silence.

From the bottom of the stairs, the phone shrilled again. Joanna raised herself onto one elbow. "No, Michael. We should answer it."

Muttering darkly, he swung his feet to the floor. When he was gone, Joanna sat up and pulled the sheet around her. She felt cold and hollow with his absence, however momentary. Still, she gave her reflection in the mirror a quick smile. Incredible as it seemed, Michael wasn't seeing anyone else. He wanted *her*. His whispered love-words still thrilled along her spine. And in a few minutes he would be back and they would continue to make love.

Of course, he hadn't actually said anything about the future, but she refused to let that concern her. She simply wouldn't let anything get in their way this time. She stared at her radiant reflection and her smile broadened. Yes. Yes!

In the few weeks they had left at the cottage, she was sure they could turn the past around.

"Jo!" Michael called urgently as he ran up the stairs. "Jo, get dressed."

"What's the matter?" she demanded as he burst into the room.

"Don't get alarmed but Casey's had an accident."

CHAPTER THIRTEEN

MICHAEL WHIPPED A SHIRT from his closet. "That was Meg on the phone. She's at the hospital with him right now."

"The hospital?" Adrenaline started pumping through Joanna's body. She jumped to her feet and ran across the hall to her room. "What kind of accident?" she called, jerking open her dresser drawer.

"Meg took the kids to some damn park this morning and apparently Casey fell off the top of a slide." He entered her room as she was still dressing.

Joanna's hands were so shaky she couldn't get the front of her dress buttoned. She had never felt so panicked in her life. Well, maybe once before, she thought as she gazed at Michael helping her button up. Poor man! He looked as frightened as she felt. He'd gone white under his tan.

"Ready?" he asked.

"No, but let's go."

Meg was sitting outside the emergency room with her three children. She looked pale and nervous. When she spotted them, she shot to her feet, swinging her littlest one onto her hip.

"Where's Casey?" Joanna burst out.

"Inside." Meg tilted her head toward one of the many doors along the corridor. "They're preparing him for X rays."

Joanna started off, but Meg held her back a moment. "Jo, I'm really sorry. I was right there, honestly. It wasn't as if I let them run around unattended."

Joanna could see the anguish she was suffering. She
would have felt the same. "Stop that right now. Accidents
happen and there's nothing we can do to stop them."

"I know, but I was so careful. I don't know what happened. He moved so fast."

"Stop feeling guilty, Meg. It's not your fault."

The baby began to whine and squirm.

"You'd better take these kids home. There's nothing else
you can do here."

But Meg shook her head. "Steve's off-island, but I called
Nathan to come get them. I'd like to stay."

"No, I insist you go, and I don't have time to argue."
Joanna looked around. Michael had already disappeared.

"Well, I gave the doctor all the information I could,
which wasn't much..."

"Then goodbye." Joanna was adamant.

A moment later, she was standing by Michael's side,
looking down at Casey's small, inert body. There was a
large gauze pad on his forehead and several scrapes on his
arms and legs. Splayed out on the harshly lit table, he
looked so small and vulnerable.

"Casey, Mommy's here," she whispered, wishing with
all her heart that she could gather him up and return him
to some sort of protective womb.

"He can't hear you, Jo," Michael said.

"Are you the boy's parents?" the doctor in attendance
asked.

Joanna looked up, distracted and frightened.

"This is the boy's mother," Michael answered for her.

The doctor was forcing Casey's eyelids open and shining a narrow flashlight into his unseeing irises. "Uh huh,"
he murmured. "Uh huh. Casey's had a bad fall." He lifted
the gauze and replaced it quickly. Joanna winced at the
sight of the gash. "He may have a sprained wrist, maybe
even a fracture, but we aren't too concerned about that at
the moment. I'm more concerned about his head." Joanna reached for Michael's hand. "I believe he's given
himself a walloping concussion." The doctor was middle-

aged, gray-haired, and smiled sympathetically. "Do worry, he'll be all right. Children come in with conc sions all the time."

Joanna stared at him numbly. Yes, but not *my* child! s wanted to shout. But she didn't. She felt too weak even move.

"You said something about X rays before Mrs. Inga came in?" Michael reminded him.

"Yes, we'll take him up in a few minutes. In the mea time, would you be so kind as to fill out a few forms, M Ingalls? I'm sure it's the last thing you feel like doing rig now, but it's hospital policy."

"Yes, of course." Joanna turned confusedly.

"At the desk in the lobby."

She nodded, giving her son a hesitant glance.

"I'll stay with him," Michael reassured her.

She nodded again, feeling like a puppet whose strin were being manipulated by some cruel fate.

She took a seat out in the hall and started to fill in t lines—Casey's name, his age and address, her name, pho number, employer... The print was swimming under h trembling pen. She found her insurance card and jotte down her identification number. Childhood diseases . Immunizations... Date of last tetanus shot? Joanna w afraid she was going to cry. Was there no end to this form And where were they wheeling Casey?

Suddenly she was aware of someone standing beside he She looked up, dropped the clipboard and rose to her fee

"Oh, Nathan! Casey—"

"I know. I heard all about it." He folded her into a warn embrace.

Joanna tensed and was glad that he released her quickly

"Have the doctors been able to give you any news on hi condition?"

"Most likely he has a concussion. They're taking him u for X rays now."

Nathan's hands were still on her arms, stroking then comfortingly. "I'm sure he'll be fine."

Suddenly she remembered why he was there. "Oh, Nathan, you shouldn't have come. Meg's already taken her
kids home."

"Oh, has she? Well, good. Now I'm free to stay with
you."

"That's very thoughtful, but Michael's here."

The expression on Nathan's rugged face fell. "Oh, I see."

"He's with Casey now."

His warm brown eyes avoided hers. "I guess you really
don't need me then."

Joanna swallowed hard. She didn't want to hurt Nathan. She liked him so much, but only as a friend.

"I'm sorry, Jo, I know this isn't the time nor place to
bring up the subject, but I was serious about wanting you
to stay here on the Vineyard. You may not have noticed, but
I happen to be crazy about you." His voice strained with
emotion.

She lowered her head. She wished she could love this man
in return. Life would be so simple then.

"I'm sorry, too. We had such a good time going out together. You made it easy for me to get back into the swing
of things. But I never meant to lead you on."

Nathan still looked hurt. Impetuously she added, "Who
knows? Maybe sometime in the future..."

He sighed resignedly. "Yeah, maybe." He paused and
glanced away. "He doesn't deserve you, y'know."

Joanna followed his gaze down the corridor to where
Michael was talking with the doctor. "Who? Michael?
There's nothing between..." But the words died of their
own weakness. Was her love for Michael that obvious to
others?

Nathan shrugged. "Oh, well, I'll be around if things
don't work out."

Joanna embraced him. "Thank you. You're quite a
friend."

He winked and disappeared in the dazzle of sunlight
outside the glass doors.

Joanna turned with a pensive frown. Michael was hurrying toward her.

"We can wait for Casey up in his room. He'll be out of X ray soon."

"His room?"

Michael nodded grimly. "They'd like to keep him over night."

Joanna picked up her handbag and began to follow.

"Mrs. Ingalls?" the secretary at the desk called. "The admission forms?"

"Oh." Joanna paused. "May I take them with me? I'd like to be with my son when he gets to his room."

The woman hesitated. "I guess it'll be okay, but please bring them down as soon as possible."

"Thanks."

Casey drifted into unconsciousness once or twice more that long afternoon. Mostly, though, he just lay there, dizzy and nauseated, his head hurting so much that sometimes he cried.

The doctor came in as supper trays were clinking down the corridor and said that Casey was lucky. "No fractured skull, Mrs. Ingalls. Just a concussion. But it's a mean one. That's why we decided to keep him overnight. I'll check on him again tomorrow, bright and early. Most likely he'll be able to go home then." In the meantime, he assured her, the nurses would take good care of him.

"May I stay?" She didn't know why she was bothering to ask. Nothing was going to pry her from Casey's side.

The doctor sighed heavily. "We can't provide a bed . . ."

"I know. A chair's fine. I'd really rather be here."

"So would I."

Joanna shot Michael a glance and knew there would be no dissuading him, either.

"Sure." The doctor nodded. "I understand."

When he was gone, Michael said he was going in search of the cafeteria. "What can I bring back for you, Jo?"

Though she wasn't the least bit hungry, she suddenly realized she hadn't eaten all day. "Soup and crackers, tea, anything."

"I'll drop this off for you at the desk, too."

Joanna looked up sharply, remembering the admission form. "Oh, don't bother. I can go down later."

"Don't be silly." The clipboard was already in his hand and he was halfway out the door. Joanna fell back into the chair, closed her eyes and whispered a silent prayer.

Joanna and Michael didn't say much as the night ticked on. They just sat and listened to the sounds drifting in from the corridor—the metallic repetition of doctors' names, the small ping of bells.

"I hate hospitals." Joanna shuddered, gazing at Michael for comfort. She was so grateful he was there.

His lips pressed together in what appeared to be a smile, but no emotion reached his eyes. He seemed lost in thought, distracted. Lines creased his brow.

"There's no need for you to stay," she said.

"I'll stay, if you don't mind." His eyes avoided hers. He had been acting strangely ever since he'd returned from the cafeteria. Still, he hadn't said anything... He was probably just as tired and worried about Casey as she was. At least, she hoped this was the reason.

They dozed in their chairs and the night passed. Casey woke shortly before dawn, crying, and a nurse gave him an injection to ease the pain of his bruises. Soon afterward, carts laden with breakfast trays rattled down the corridor. Outside the sun was growing hot and life was resuming as usual, but not in here. Joanna felt time had stopped within these sterile walls.

She gazed at Michael. His shirt was rumpled, and his cheeks were shadowed by a day's growth of beard. He did indeed look tired and worried, yet every time she'd asked him how he was, he'd said fine. Evidently his fondness for Casey ran deeper than she had ever suspected.

A nurse came in and for the hundredth time, it seemed, checked his pulse and eyes. "Nothing we can do really. In

a situation like this, the body mends itself in its own goo
time. Let him rest. He's doing fine.''

"Where am I?" Casey asked when she was gone, his blu
eyes looking too large for his tiny face.

"At the hospital, kid," Michael answered softly, lea
'ing close. "Do you remember what happened yesterday ;
the park?"

Casey shook his head and winced with the sudden pai
it caused.

"You fell off a slide, honey," Joanna offered, wo
riedly.

"Oh, yeah. I wanted to go down on my stomach, so
stood up to turn around and—"

"Oh, Casey!" Joanna admonished softly.

"I won't do it again, Ma."

"I'm sure you won't." Michael leaned over and kisse
the boy's head tenderly.

Joanna ducked into the bathroom so Casey wouldn't se
the tears that were welling in her bloodshot eyes.

When she returned, Michael was reading Casey a stor
from a book borrowed from the playroom down the hall
He leaned heavily on the bed, his eyes half-closed.

"You look worse than he does," she said, trying to sound
cheerful. "Why don't you go grab yourself some coffee?"

Michael didn't protest. In fact, he didn't say anything t
her at all, only to Casey. "I'll be back soon, kid. Don't g
out dancing while I'm gone." The child giggled weakly.

Casey was released that afternoon. Despite her exhaus
tion, Joanna felt almost light with relief. He would have to
rest quietly for a few days, and she would have to watch for
any signs of recurring nausea or blurred vision, but the
worst was over. He would soon be as good as new.

Michael carried him into the living room and laid him on
the couch. "Would you like me to turn on the TV?"

Casey nodded.

"Okay, you and Bugs keep each other company for a
while. I'm going up to shower, and then I've got to go out,
but I'll be back real soon."

"Where are you going?" Joanna stopped him as he headed for the stairs.

He turned but didn't quite raise his eyes to hers. "Just to pick up a few things." He had been unusually quiet since Casey's accident. He'd said so little to her directly that she was sure he was avoiding her on purpose. She wished she could attribute it to tiredness, but she knew it wasn't that. He had simply retreated into himself and was brooding on...on something. It hurt to be cut out of his life this abruptly, especially after the intimacy they had come to share. But where was that closeness now when she needed it most? Was their relationship so fragile that it had already broken? And why? What had she done?

Meg dropped by some time later with a platter of macaroni salad and slices of ham and cheese. "I figured you wouldn't be in much of a mood to cook," she explained. She also brought get-well cards from her children.

Joanna was glad of her visit. After the tension of the past two days, she needed someone as talkative and jolly as Meg. When she left, Joanna felt immeasurably better.

After an early supper, she tucked Casey into bed with a favorite stuffed toy, then lowered the window against the damp ocean breeze. Twilight obscured the road until it was just a trench of darkness cut into the jungle of beach plum and bayberry. In the distance, faintly luminescent, was the twisting path of sand that cut through to the beach. The ocean was calm tonight, the low breaking waves just a murmur.

Her vacation was more than half over. The sun was already setting noticeably sooner than it had just a few weeks ago. There were brilliant bars of vermilion streaking the evening sky. Somewhere over the rolling meadows, a robin trilled his last plaintive song of the day.

Joanna felt her heart swell with emotion. How she loved this place! And how dearly she loved the man who was sharing it with her. If only the summer didn't have to end....

But end it would. In three short weeks her vacatio
would be over. And then what? Would Michael ask her t
stay on with him? For a moment she felt a surge of opt
mism, the same hope she had allowed herself to feel onl
days ago. But it soon crumpled under the weight of doub
Michael was acting so strangely...

Suddenly Joanna felt depressed and frightened. Sh
dreaded going back to New Hampshire. She hadn't th
slightest inclination toward returning to the store or be
coming a computer programmer. At that moment she sa
herself with a clarity that was startling. What she wante
most out of life was to be Michael's wife, to be his mate til
the end of her days.

It really didn't matter where they lived or what the
worked at—just as long as they were together. Everythin
else was secondary and would fall into place.

But living here on the Vineyard would be ideal. In
house not too different from this one, only larger to ac
commodate the other children they would surely have. And
there would have to be a study where Michael could ge
away to write...and a garden where she could grow her
flowers.

Joanna smiled ruefully. In a world where women wer
battling to free themselves from the role of housewife and
mother, here she was wishing desperately for just the op
posite.

Not that she ruled out the possibility of working, too, a
long as the work was satisfying and meshed with her fam
ily life. Work like the typing she'd done for Michael. Yes,
she'd enjoy working at home, making her own hours, set
ting her own goals. Maybe she could start a typing service
with a good word processor, maybe she could even get into
small publications...

But, of course, she was letting her mind wander ludi-
crously. She was dealing in dreams, dreams made possible
only in some uncomplicated and ideal world—and the real
world was anything but! In fact, she had bowed to expe-
diency so often in the past that her life was now a mud hole

f complications. And if she knew what was good for her-
elf and Casey, she would go on sloshing through.

"Night, Casey. If you need me, just call. I'll be down on
he porch." He smiled dreamily, his eyelids lifting slightly
hen falling again into sleep.

Michael was sitting at the top of the wooden stairs that
ed down the bluff to the dock. Joanna hadn't been aware
hat he'd returned. She hesitated for a moment, then gave
n and joined him.

She settled down on the step beside him, drew up her
:nees, and tucked her midcalf skirt around her ankles.
"Hi," she said nervously.

Michael continued to gaze out over the dark water, his
ong, graceful hands pressed to his lips in thought.

"Have you eaten?" Joanna hoped she could somehow
draw him out of his sullen mood.

But he probably hadn't even heard her. "How's Casey?"

"Fine. Asleep."

He nodded pensively, dropped his hands between his
knees and took a deep breath. "Jo, may I ask you a question?"

"Sure."

"How much did Casey weigh when he was born?"

"What?" she laughed. Just as abruptly, however, she
went very still. "I don't remember."

Michael turned his head and pinned her with a cold, la-
serlike stare. "All right, let me put it this way—was Casey
premature?"

Joanna suddenly felt numb. She had a sense of everything in her past rushing up on her, all the days and months
and years since she'd run away from this cottage leading to
this appointed place and time. *Lie!* she told herself. For
heaven's sake, lie!

But Michael was looking right through her, and she
couldn't even breathe.

CHAPTER FOURTEEN

"ANSWER ME, dammit!" Michael exploded.

Joanna jumped. "All right! All right!" she snapped, h[i] anger grating on her already traumatized nerves. There wa nowhere to run, nothing to do but face the moment she' hoped would never come. Somehow he'd found out an[y] way. "He wasn't premature. Casey was a perfectly health seven pounds, ten ounces."

"Then . . . he was conceived that summer?"

She swallowed hard. She couldn't answer but Micha[e] could read her expression. He covered his eyes with hi hand.

Joanna was beginning to feel sick. She touched his ar[m] but he flung her off and turned away.

"H-how did you find out?" she asked shakily.

It took a while before Michael could speak. He cleare[d] his throat. "I saw his date of birth on the hospital admis sion form you filled out."

Joanna nodded. She'd known that was a mistake, let ting him take that form to the desk. Up to now she'd bee[n] so careful . . .

"So, little Casey is my son. *My* son." He stared up at the grayness of approaching night as if searching for some thing that would help him understand what he'd just said. His expression hardened. "Jo, how could you keep him from me all these years? How could you do that to me? All this time . . . Did I mean so little to you? Did you hate me that much?"

Joanna had feared this would be Michael's reaction, right from the day she had decided to keep Casey's patern-

y a secret. Over the years her fear had only grown. The
onger she kept the secret, the angrier he would be when he
ound out. *If* he found out. But he never would, she had
hought.

"Michael, once a deception is started, it's awfully hard
o go back," she began vaguely. "Besides, there was Phil.
He wanted to raise Casey with no interference from an-
ther party."

Michael turned. "He knew?"

Inside, she felt as if she were dying. "Yes. He asked me
o promise I'd never tell. And then there was Casey him-
elf," she added quickly. "I didn't want him growing up
orn and confused, like I did."

"Still, you could have found a way," he persisted. "Even
f you never told him I was his father, you could have had
me meet him and get to know him." He wasn't just angry;
Michael was hurting, hurting deeply. "You can't imagine
now frustrated I feel right now. I'm so angry, so sad...and
there's nothing I can do...all that wasted time! And the
saddest part is, that time's gone forever. Nothing can bring
it back. It's lost to me."

Joanna nodded. Now, when she loved him more than her
own life, Michael loathed her. And she didn't blame him.
Keeping a son from his father, concealing the fact of that
son's very existence, robbing the father of all the joy of
those infant and toddler years, that was unforgivable—an
enormous wound that refused to heal.

Michael continued to stare out over the water. "Why
didn't you tell me you were pregnant?"

Joanna didn't know what to say.

"Damn you, Joanna! Why didn't you tell me?"

His renewed anger startled her. "I didn't know it myself, not till after I left here."

"Why didn't you get in touch with me then?"

Joanna gasped in disbelief and felt anger rising inside
her, too. "I might not have been too smart, but I wasn't a
masochist. You already had a pregnant girlfriend, or so we

all believed at the time, and you'd made the decision
marry her."

"No, I hadn't." Then he paused and looked at her que
tioningly. "But I hadn't! Who told you that?"

"Everybody. My father. Your mother. Don't try to r;
tionalize your way out of it now. Furthermore, if yo
weren't planning to marry Bunny, why didn't you try :
contact *me*?"

"I did! For weeks!"

They stared hard at each other. Joanna felt angry an
hurt, but all at once she realized she was also very cor
fused. "I'm getting a bad feeling about all this, Michael,
she whispered, sitting very still.

"Me, too. Me, too." The pensive lines returned to h
brow. "*Where* did you say you went after you left here?"

"Home, of course. But my mother suspected somethin
had happened here. She kept asking me questions an
started going through my things. So I left for school."

"School?"

"Yes. You remember. I was supposed to be going to co
lege that fall? Classes weren't starting for another week, bu
the dorm was open and I moved in. I had to be alone."

"Is *that* where you were?" He turned to face her mor
directly. "I called your house so many times, but you
mother just kept saying you weren't there."

Joanna's eyes widened. "You really called?"

"Mmm. I guess I shouldn't have told her who I was. She
didn't think she owed me any favors."

"Not with you being Vivien's son!"

"Boy, you people know how to hold a grudge!"

"You really called?"

"Of course. Joanna, did you actually think I wouldn't?"
She shrugged and Michael's look narrowed. "You mean,
all these years your mother never told you?"

"Never breathed a word."

He stared at her incredulously. "What could you possibly have been thinking? Don't answer that. I think I know.
Get back to your story. You were in college..." But again

e paused. "Why the hell were you in college if you and Phil were planning all along to get married?"

Joanna dropped her head to her knees. "We *weren't* planning to get married," she wailed. "I just happened to be pregnant and in need of a husband, and you...you were oo busy marrying somebody else to bother." Tears burned n her eyes. She could feel her composure slipping.

"But..." Michael looked confused.

"But what, Michael? You had one hell of a summer for yourself. Hell, not one, but two ladies pregnant as a result. Sorry if I don't congratulate you, Michael, but I happened o be the pregnant lady who got left out in the cold."

"Shut up!" He gripped her arm and dug his fingers into the soft flesh. "Let's get one thing straight. I loved you, loved you more than I'd loved anyone before in my life, and God only knows why but I've never loved anyone in quite the same way since."

Joanna couldn't breathe. She stared at him, tumbling dizzily into the turbulent depths of his cobalt eyes. "Well, you sure picked a fine way to show it!"

His grip tightened. "Joanna, I *never* cheated on you! Never!"

"Sure. I know. Bunny wasn't really pregnant but you thought she was—and you married her. Doesn't that sound a little fishy to you?"

Michael let her go and turned his eyes back on the dark rippled pond. "Not even you believe me," he muttered. "Don't you realize how in love with you I was? That winter before we got here...I should have known...all I lived for were your letters. And then that summer, that was the most incredible time in my life. You were so—*beautiful*."

"I was very young and naive," she bit out.

"Yes, you were. But so was I."

"Michael, you were never young."

"I was only twenty-two."

Joanna glanced away at the lights shimmering across the water from other docks and houses. "Well, whatever you felt, it was nothing compared to what I felt for you. You

had me right there!'' She thrust her palm forward. ''Righ
there! I was riding so high that summer because of yo
I . . . I . . .'' Suddenly her angry confession conjured up im
ages that were too vivid. A sob choked her. Then another
She broke down under the weight of all they'd confesse
and cried uncontrollably.

Michael stroked her back gently, then finally pulled he
closer. She buried her face in his shirt.

''Oh, Joanna, how could we have been so stupid! Hov
did we let all this happen?'' His hand caressed the side o
her face. ''Will you please tell me exactly what happene
that night? It's time we straightened this mess out.''

''Whi-ich night?''

''The night I had to go over to the Wilcoxes. The nigh
you left. Start at the beginning.''

''Oh. Well, I waited for you to come home. I suspectec
something was awfully wrong, otherwise I would have beer
included. But then only my father and Viv came back
around eleven-thirty . . .''

''And they told you the news about Bunny, that she wa:
pregnant and had accused me of being the father?''

''No, they told me you *were* the father.''

''Damn! I told them not to say anything to you. I knew
they'd distort things.''

''Then why didn't you come home?''

''Obviously, I should have. So much damage was
done . . .''

''You're darn right!'' She drew back. ''Do you have any
idea how I felt? Can you even begin to imagine how hurt I
was?''

Michael's face constricted.

''I was devastated, Michael. I was so hurt and angry I
wanted to die. I kept thinking of how close we'd been,
about the plans we'd made to get married, and I couldn't
understand how you could be so deceptive, so cruel. I
ended up hating you that night. I never wanted to see you
again. So, before the sun was even up, I packed my bags
and left the island.''

"You should have waited for me," he answered, his voice rasping with a matching pain.

"Why? What was there for me to wait for? Vivien had already said you'd agreed to marry Bunny."

"But I hadn't. She had no right to say that. It was she and Bunny's mother who brought up the subject of marriage. My mother always was a little too impressed by those people. Her fondest dream was to see me marry into that family." He drifted into a moment of reflective silence before continuing.

"I sat on the beach most of that night thinking about my predicament. The deck did seem stacked against me, Jo. You see, I'd . . . been with Bunny once, earlier in the summer."

Joanna sent him a look of pure dismay.

"It's not what you're thinking, Jo. Granted, Bunny and I had dated the summer before and, yes, I'd even made the mistake of sleeping with her. At the time, though, I thought I was in love. But, believe me, the moment passed quickly. We broke up that fall. The relationship was over well before you and I came to the Vineyard that summer. She was a part of my life before I started loving you."

"Then how do you explain that *one* time you were together? A slip of memory?"

He raked a hand through his hair in frustration. "It was early June. Like me, she'd just graduated from college, and her parents were throwing a big party for her. I didn't feel like going. I'd tried to make a clean break with her, but I knew she never really accepted it. As far as she was concerned, we were still an item, and I would come to my senses eventually and agree.

"I'd like to think she was still just infatuated with me, that her attitude sprang from purely romantic notions, but it didn't. Truth was, she just couldn't tolerate the idea of someone breaking up with her. How dare I! Nobody dumped Bunny Wilcox!

"So, anyway, there was this graduation party. I hadn't seen nor heard from her in months and I really didn't want

to go. But my mother insisted. She said the Wilcoxes would
be hurt if I didn't. As it turned out, I should have listened
to my instincts.

"The evening began with Bunny hanging all over me a
if we were long-lost lovers. Then our parents, in front o
half of Back Bay Boston, started making not-so-subtle
comments about how we were now free to make plans fo
the future. And then, I swear, Jo, I only had two drinks
but I got really sick...dizzy, headachey. I probably
shouldn't have had even one drink. I'd really pushed my
self studying for finals and still hadn't recovered. In fact
I'd been so concerned about it that I'd gone to the doctor's
that day to see if I had mono. But I didn't...just old-
fashioned exhaustion.

"I asked Bunny if she could get me some aspirin, but
after I took it I continued to feel sick. Worse even. To make
a long story short, the next thing I remember is waking up
in their guest room the next morning—with Bunny lying
beside me. I got up and left immediately.

"I didn't see her again till we were on the Vineyard. I was
positive nothing had happened that night in her guest
room, so even though I was pretty ticked off, I wasn't worried about it—not till I got called over to their cottage at the
end of the summer and she accused me of being the father
of the baby she was carrying. I told her she was crazy, I'd
been too sick to make love to anyone. There was no way
that baby—that fictional baby—could have been mine. But
nobody believed me. I don't think they wanted to. I finally
stormed out and, as I said, spent the night on the beach.

"In the morning I went back to Bunny's house all fired
up again and ready to tell her to find some other sap to
marry. I'd just remembered that when I'd woken up that
morning in their guest room, I was still wearing all my
clothes. It was a foolhardy thing to do, knowing how ex-
plosive her father can be, but, as I said, I was young and far
from prudent. Anyway, he and I argued and before I knew
what hit me, I was on my back in the middle of their liv-
ing-room rug with a broken nose."

Joanna let out a small cry. "Oh, no! The two of you fought?"

"Oh, yes!" He smiled ruefully. "Mrs. Wilcox insisted on driving me to the hospital, and by the time I was bandaged up and back here, you were long gone. I couldn't believe it—you, abandoning me, heading for high ground when the water was running up to my chin! I figured you just didn't care enough to help me through my trouble."

"Michael, how could you think that?"

"Well, what was I supposed to think? Nobody said otherwise—your father, my mother. They were obsessed with Bunny and the fact that I *had* to marry her; I *had* to do the proper thing.

"There was nothing for me to do but leave. I packed and went back to Boston. After stewing in my anger for another day, I called your house, but your mother hung up on me. I called night and day for the next two days, in fact. Then, frantic with worry, I drove up to New Hampshire."

Joanna closed her eyes against the throbbing darkness. She didn't think she wanted to hear this. A truth was emerging, a truth she didn't want to face. If only she'd stayed and waited, the smoke would have cleared eventually. And how different her life would have been! How different it would be now! She should have trusted Michael more. That's what marriages were built on.

"I went to your house and encountered the iron lady you call your mother," Michael continued with a grimace. "Though I don't suppose she told you any more about that than she did about my phone calls?"

Joanna shook her head. "She hated everything associated with my father and Viv, and that included you."

"I guess I scared the hell out of her, too." He laughed bitterly. "I hadn't shaved in about five days, hadn't slept. I looked like a derelict, with a bandage over my nose and two black eyes. The first day I showed up at her door, she told me you'd gone away for a while and couldn't be reached. The second day, she told me in no uncertain terms to buzz off. The third day, she had the telephone in her hand and threatened to call the police.''

In spite of her misery, Joanna chuckled. "She would have, too.''

"I didn't doubt it even then. At that point, I was already a day late for my presemester curriculum meetings, so I drove back to Boston, packed up, and headed down to Virginia.''

Joanna calculated the days on her fingers. "That was just about the time I was calling Phil.''

Michael's dark head tilted, and she could see the pained curiosity in his eyes,.

"As I told you, I was living in the dorm waiting for classes to start and...and I was beginning to suspect something was wrong. So, I went to a clinic and had myself tested. Sure enough, I was pregnant. Well, let me tell you, I didn't know which way to turn. I wasn't about to tell my mother. She would have had a stroke, especially if she found out you were the father. And I certainly couldn't go back to my father. So I called Phil. He was my best friend.''

"Was he only that? I know you two had dated.''

"Yes, we'd dated. I...I think he always loved me.''

"And you?''

"I liked Phil immensely. He was kind, steady, gentle. We practically grew up together. But I didn't always love him. That didn't come until later...after we were married. When I called him from school, he was just a friend.

"Well, as soon as we got off the phone, Phil drove up to school with a solution to my problem. He offered to marry me and raise the baby as his own. When it was born, we would simply tell our folks it was premature.''

"Did he know I was the father?''

"Yes. He was aware of the whole situation right from the beginning.''

"That explains it then." Michael chewed thoughtfully on his lower lip.

"Explains what?''

"I went back to New Hampshire as soon as my preliminary business at school was straightened out."

"Again?"

"Mmm, I had a few free days before the actual start of classes. I went back to see your mother, and this time she told me where I could find you. I couldn't believe it. She gave me an address, and I went racing over to an apartment above a store."

Joanna's lips parted mutely.

"That's right. She sent me over to your apartment. Or rather to what would be your apartment in a couple of weeks. Someone was there, all right, but it wasn't you. It was Phil. He was painting a ceiling." Michael paused and his eyes grew sad. "I introduced myself and he gave me the strangest look, but, of course, now I understand it. You had told him all about me and what a rat I was."

Joanna didn't deny it.

"I asked for you but he was evasive—said you were out shopping and didn't know when you'd be back. Told me he was getting the apartment ready for you. And then he hit me with the news that you were going to be married. I was knocked off my feet. I didn't believe him at first, not till he showed me around the place and I saw your things."

Joanna's head was swimming. Michael had once been in her apartment?

He grew quiet, pensive. "Can you imagine how I felt, seeing boxes of your clothing...the blue sweater I loved so much lying across the bed..."

Joanna touched his arm, but he wouldn't be comforted. He turned away from her instead, hunched forward as if protecting a pain he'd grown accustomed to.

"What could I say to him? I felt like such a damn fool! So I said nothing, not about you, not about our summer or our plans for the future. Nothing. I just stood there, confused and bleeding...."

"Please don't be angry at Phil...."

Michael dropped his head and shook it side to side. "No. Of course not. He undoubtedly saw himself as your knight in shining armor, fighting to rescue your pride. And me—I was the villain.

"I told him I thought your marriage was rather sudden, and without taking a second to think, he contradicted me. Not at all, he said. The two of you went all the way back to the fourth grade. You had always intended to get married." Michael's expression became sad and wistful. "He must have really loved you, Jo, the way he covered for you, knowing I was the father of the baby he was going to raise! I told him I thought you two were awfully young to be getting married and that it was a mistake. But he was ready for me again. He said age had nothing to do with making mistakes and at least you were making yours out of free choice. That hit me like a ton of bricks. I realized then that you must have told him all about me and Bunny, and maybe you were laughing at my predicament."

"No! Never!"

"Well, I was so confused I didn't know what to think. I wished the two of you well and left the apartment. I never went back after that. I figured there was no use. The Wilcoxes, meanwhile, were making arrangements for a wedding and, well, I went along with them. Bunny needed a husband, or so I thought, and maybe I had slept with her after all. I wasn't sure of anything at that point. And, well, it just didn't matter anymore what I did. It didn't matter..." His voice trailed off into a thin thread of remembered despair.

Even while Joanna watched him, though, his expression hardened. "But of course, I hadn't slept with her. After her pretend miscarriage, I forced her to level with me. She had made up the whole story. And the reason I don't remember being put to bed in their guest room—those two aspirins she gave me were really her mother's Valium! Ten milligrams of the stuff, on top of alcohol and exhaustion!"

"That idiot! She could have done you so much more harm!"

They fell into a long, sad silence. Finally Joanna looked up, smiling wanly. "Do you know who we remind me of?"

"Who?"

"Romeo and Juliet. We were running on blind impetuosity, missing each other at all the most crucial moments."

Michael began to nod.

"We were surrounded by well-meaning people, too," she continued, "just like they were, who in the end did more damage than good."

Now he shook his head. "When it came to us, nobody was well-meaning. They were too caught up in their own myopic bitterness. And the damage they did runs so deep it can never be repaired."

The weak smile on Joanna's lips quivered. No, it probably never could. In the same moment she also realized that their whole conversation had revolved on the love they *used* to feel for each other. "I loved you more than anyone else," he had said, but not once had he said that he loved her still. They could clear the air, iron out misconceptions, illuminate the past till everything was perfectly explained. But the fact remained: whatever love he had felt for her, however true or passionate or exclusive, it was all a part of the past.

CHAPTER FIFTEEN

"Do you want to move inside?" Michael suggested, noticing Joanna shiver. "It's getting a little damp."

"Yes. I'd like to be closer to Casey, too."

In the sun porch, Michael settled into his favorite chair while Joanna lit the candle in the hurricane lamp between them. Its steady glow drew them into a circle of intimacy carved out of the warm, dark night.

She sat and folded her hands. There was nothing more to say about their disaster-riddled past. But the conversation wasn't over yet. They still had to face the issue at the heart of it all—Casey.

She chanced a look at Michael. He was holding his hands to his mouth, prayerlike, his stare never wavering from her face. Candlelight flickered in his eyes and cast shadows over the planes of his high-boned cheeks.

"So, Casey is my son," he said finally, his voice contemplative and slow. Joanna nodded, barely able to swallow past the tightening in her throat. "You've done a fine job of raising him."

"You think so?"

"Sure. He's a wonderful child. Bright, happy, well behaved . . ."

"He looks exactly like you." Immediately she wished she'd kept the thought to herself. Michael's expression crumbled into a look of raw grief. She knew he was thinking again about all the years he had missed with Casey.

"You could have found a way," she thought she heard him mutter before he got up from his chair. For a long time he stood at the screen door, lost in the blackness of the night.

Joanna felt unutterably miserable. Those missing years evidently canceled out everything that had happened between them this summer—the happiness, the working together, the glorious lovemaking. How stupid it had been of her to start hoping, to start thinking they had a chance! Michael loathed her for keeping Casey a secret! Had she thought he would never find out? And even if he never did, did she think they could be truly happy with such a grave deception over their heads?

"I guess it's silly to say we can make it right," she murmured sadly. "As silly as trying to turn back time."

"Yes, it is. The past is lost to us," he agreed. "But I'd like to do something about the future, Jo."

Joanna's head snapped up. "What did you say?"

"I'd like to see Casey regularly from now on."

She smiled—until his words registered. "Oh, I see."

He turned. "Is that all right with you?"

"Yes, sure. He's grown very fond of you." Why had she just let herself think he might want to include her in that future? She knew how deeply he was hurt.

"You don't have to worry about my confusing him, either. I won't breathe a word about our relationship till he's old enough to handle it."

Joanna nodded woodenly, feeling bereft. She pushed herself up from the chair with a sudden longing to be alone. "Sad, isn't it?" she said softly.

"What is?"

"That we have the capacity to understand how and where and why we went wrong—but not the capacity to forgive." Her chin sank to her chest as she stumbled into the house.

If only she'd introduced Michael to Casey sooner, perhaps by now the sting would be gone. But that would have been impossible. How could she have arranged to have Michael visit without turning her marriage into a battleground? For that matter, how was she going to cope with his visits now? How would she greet him at the door? What

small talk would they make? How could she bottle up a
the love inside without letting it tear her apart? And wha
if he came to see Casey with another woman—or worse,
wife? How would she smile and wish them well?

No, she couldn't do it. She'd have to arrange it so tha
Michael came to visit Casey when she wasn't around. Sh
couldn't bear to see him anymore. It would kill her slowl
but surely if she did.

In the dark, she slipped out of her clothes and into a long
cotton nightgown. Casey was sleeping restfully.

She glimpsed her wan, dejected reflection in the bath
room mirror and thought again about going home. Thi
time she meant to go through with it. There was a sense o
morbidity to the cottage now. As long as she and Michae
remained here together, grief would be with them. She had
to leave.

Michael had just reached the top of the stairs when she
left the bathroom. She looked down at the floor as he
walked past her on his way to his room.

"Michael?" she called impulsively. "I'm thinking of
going home tomorrow."

He turned to gaze at her, his eyes narrowed. "That's not
necessary, Jo."

"Yes, it is. Trying to share this place now would be a
farce."

He swallowed, looking uncomfortable. "Is Casey ready
to travel?"

She shook her head. "I was wondering if you'd like to
keep him here with you for a few weeks."

"Just the two of us?"

"Uh huh. It'll give you guys a chance to make up a little
of that lost time." Though she smiled, she could feel her
jaw trembling. "I'll come pick him up at the end of August."

Michael nodded slowly. "I'd like that." He took a step
away from her, then paused again. "What are *you* going to
do in the meantime?"

She shrugged. "Go back to New Hampshire, look for a new apartment, work . . . same old grind."

He nodded again, and they continued to move apart, but more slowly.

"Oh, by the way," Michael added, "Doug McCrory loves my novel."

Joanna's eyes flew wide open. "What?"

He nodded without emotion. "I called Joyce today while I was out. She gave him the finished manuscript Saturday night at her party and he read it the next day."

"The publisher?"

"Mmm. He had to find out what Joyce was raving about. Raving, apparently, isn't her normal mode of doing business."

"And he loves it?"

Michael nodded.

Joanna studied his crestfallen face a moment. "What's the matter? Aren't they paying you enough?"

He laughed ironically. "They're paying me quite well, thank you."

"Then what's wrong?"

"Nothing you'd understand." He sighed as he reached for the doorknob, but then he paused. His mouth tightened and he began to blink rapidly. "Joanna, don't go."

Her breath caught in her throat. "W-what did you say?"

He rested his head against the door, as though he were drained of strength. "Please. Stay here."

Joanna hesitated, wondering if her heart still remembered how to beat. Surely he couldn't be saying what she thought he was!

Slowly he lifted his head and looked at her, a man disarmed. "I should be really happy now. I've finally established the career of my dreams, I've become financially independent. . . . But something is still wrong." His deep baritone wavered. "I still feel incomplete, as if half of me is missing. Joanna?" He lifted a hand, reaching out to her. "I need you with me."

With clamoring heart, she ran into his arms. He gathered her close and held her tight. They were both trembling.

"Jo, we've made a lot of mistakes in the past and we've both been hurt, but that's no reason for us to go on punishing ourselves the rest of our lives." They clung to each other as if they were afraid to let go. Finally their trembling subsided; their bodies relaxed and they drew slightly apart.

Michael caressed her face, stroked back her tangled hair. "There's still so much between us, Jo."

She wanted desperately to believe him, but how could she be certain he wasn't going to hurt her again? "What you mean is, there's still a physical attraction between us."

He surveyed her fearful expression. "Oh, yes, there's still that."

Joanna swallowed painfully. Should she tell him she was sorry, but a physical relationship wasn't enough? Or should she be silent? Didn't she love Michael so much she would take him on any terms?

"But a physical attraction isn't all there is between us, and you know it!" He guided her into his room and closed the door, pinning her against it with his body. "I love you, Joanna. I *love* you. You're... you're my soul, my body's breath, my life's joy."

Joanna wound her arms around his neck and drew his head down so that their eyes were level. "Wherever we go, whatever we do..." She could feel her throat tightening with tears. "And I love you, Michael."

His lips quivered for a second. "Good. That's all that really matters, you know—not how many years we've spent apart, not who we've been with or who hurt whom—just our love, now and in the future." He kissed her forehead tenderly. His hands stroked her arms and came to rest on her hips. He urged her closer. "Jo, will you marry me?"

She melted into his embrace. A tear spilled down her cheek.

"You probably think I'm an awful risk. I mean, a man who loves writing so much he gives up his job and apartment for it, lives on the beach like a transient. But—"

Joanna placed a finger over his lips. "I'd marry you if you were a pauper."

"But that's what I'm trying to explain. I'm not a pauper. Gateway is offering me a contract for my next three novels!"

"Are you kidding me?" she shrieked, forgetting Casey was asleep across the hall.

"No! And the terms are phenomenal! I already have an outline for one story, and I have ..." Suddenly he paused. "Hey, what did you say?"

"About what?"

"Did I hear you say you *would* marry me?"

"Sure did." She felt a smile tugging at her mouth. She began to unbutton his shirt. "When would you like to do it?"

"Tomorrow? Or is that too soon?"

"Don't you want to plan a reception or anything?" she asked. "Invite a few people, like our parents?"

"No! Especially not them!"

"Michael, they're our parents. Besides, they're responsible for our getting together this summer."

"By mistake."

Joanna's hands roamed over his chest, her fingers sliding through the mat of his coarse, dark hair. "The loveliest mistake they ever made," she whispered huskily.

"Yes, I suppose you're right." He began to smile. "We'll have them here for a visit—but not until we've tied the knot good and tight. I'm not taking any chances this time!"

Joanna smiled too. Her hands glided down to his hips and rock-hard thighs. She could feel desire rising through his tautening body, and it thrilled her to know she had the power to move such a virile man as Michael.

"Oh, well," she sighed, abruptly drawing away. "Now that's settled, I'd better be getting back to my room. If Casey wakes up, he'll wonder where I am."

Michael's eyes gleamed with desire for her. A smile tilte
his mouth. "You're not going anywhere and you know i
And as far as my son is concerned, he's just going to hav
to get used to looking for you in my bed in the mornin
because that's where you're going to be from now on, ever
morning, for the rest of our lives."

JOANNA FELL into a deep peaceful sleep after they mad
love, but she woke again just before dawn. Thin gray ligh
was easing through the open windows. Gulls were begin
ning to caw above the ocean's soft murmur. She gazed lov
ingly at Michael, still asleep beside her.

She felt incredibly content. It amazed her to think tha
she had come to this cottage on Martha's Vineyard just five
weeks ago feeling drained of every ounce of hope or en
thusiasm. Everything important in life seemed to be be
hind her. And now, here she was, profoundly happy,
realizing that life was just beginning. So much lay ahead of
her.

She and Michael had rediscovered their summer love,
and this time she knew nothing would ever come between
them. Theirs was a special kind of love, an enduring love,
one that would take them through all the seasons of their
lives.

HARLEQUIN
Romance®

Coming Next Month

#3073 BLUEBIRDS IN THE SPRING Jeanne Allan
After the death of her mother and stepfather, Tracy could have done without a
bodyguard—especially Neil Charles. Attractive but arrogant, he clearly held Tracy's
wealthy image in contempt. They sparred constantly but she fell in love with him just
the same.

#3074 TRUST ME, MY LOVE Sally Heywood
Though it went against her nature, Tamsin had every incentive to deceive Jake Newman
on her employer's behalf. Yet when it came to the crunch, she found that Jake's trust in
her was the only thing that mattered.

#3075 PLACE FOR THE HEART Catherine Leigh
Florida real-estate developer Felicity Walden knows the Dubois family's Wyoming ranch
would make a perfect vacation resort—but Beau Dubois refuses to sell. Still, she's
convinced that a cowboy's stubbornness is no match for an Easterner's determination.
Even though the cowboy is far too handsome for the Easterner's peace of mind....

#3076 RAINY DAY KISSES Debbie Macomber
Susannah Simmons knows what she wants—career success at any cost. Until she falls in
love with Nate Townsend. But her five-year plan doesn't leave room for romance,
especially with a man who seems to reject all the values Susannah prizes so highly.

#3077 PASSPORT TO HAPPINESS Jessica Steele
Jayme should have been devastated when she found her fiancé in another woman's arms.
But there was no time to brood over the past. She was too busy coping with presently
being stranded in Italy in the hands of attractive Nerone Mondadori....

#3078 JESTER'S GIRL Kate Walker
The moment he set foot in her restaurant, Daniel Tyson antagonized Jessica Terry.
Though she reacted to him as a stranger, there were two things she didn't know. One was
Daniel's unusual occupation; the other was that they'd met—and fought—once before.

**Available in September wherever paperback books are sold, or
through Harlequin Reader Service:**

In the U.S.
901 Fuhrmann Blvd.
P.O. Box 1397
Buffalo, N.Y. 14240-1397

In Canada
P.O. Box 603
Fort Erie, Ontario
L2A 5X3

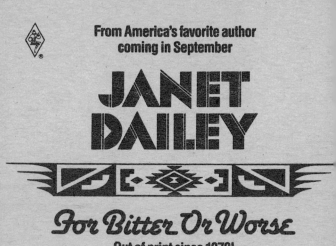

HARLEQUIN
American Romance®

THE LOVES OF A CENTURY...

Join American Romance in a nostalgic look back at the Twentieth Century—at the lives and loves of American men and women from the turn-of-the-century to the dawn of the year 2000.

Journey through the decades from the dance halls of the 1900s to the discos of the seventies ... from Glenn Miller to the Beatles ... from Valentino to Newman ... from corset to miniskirt ... from beau to Significant Other.

Relive the moments ... recapture the memories.

Look now for the CENTURY OF AMERICAN ROMANCE series in Harlequin American Romance. In one of the four American Romance titles appearing each month, for the next twelve months, we'll take you back to a decade of the Twentieth Century, where you'll relive the years and rekindle the romance of days gone by.

Don't miss a day of the CENTURY OF AMERICAN ROMANCE.

A CENTURY OF
AMERICAN ROMANCE
1900's

The women...the men...the passions... the memories....

CAR-1